Give Him Back 2

Kemp & Satin

B.M. Hardin

ISBN-13: 978-1726490160
ISBN-10: 1726490165

This book is a work of fiction. Any similarities of people, places, instances, and locals, are coincidental and solely a work of the authors imagination.

Dear Readers

Honestly, I didn't expect this book to do as well as it has! I want to thank all of you for taking this journey with me. I appreciate every purchase, every download, every share, mention, recommendation, and review. I appreciate your support. More than you will ever know! Thank you!

Join My BRAND NEW Facebook Group at the end of the book!

In Loving Memory of

Lisa Fleming

Give Him Back 2

Chapter One

SATIN

Coming back here was a mistake.

I knew it.

I could feel it.

But I wasn't sure if Kemp could feel it too.

I had this strange feeling that when it was all said and done someone was going to end up hurt...or dead.

And I wasn't talking about our next target.

I was referring to Kemp...or Lava.

And for the first time ever, I would be the one holding the smoking gun.

Kemp looked at me with a smirk. "What are you talking about, babe?"

"Are you going to see her while we're here?"

"Who?"

"You know who! Lava?" I growled.

Kemp laughed lightly, as though he was amused. "No, I don't plan on seeing her. I don't even know how long it takes to get to her from here."

"So?"

"So, that means chill the hell out. Okay?"

I exhaled loudly and rolled my eyes.

He could say whatever he wanted to say, but I knew the truth. He still felt something for her. He might even love her.

I couldn't be sure, but it was something.

Something about her that he just couldn't shake. No matter how hard he tried to hide it.

I couldn't count the number of times I'd glanced at his phone to see him scrolling down the newsfeeds of her social media. Or the times I would catch him in a daze, only for a look of guilt to spread across his face once he noticed me standing there.

I'm pretty sure he would be thinking about her.

"We're here to work. That's it. We didn't dish out all that money and have someone else take the blame for the bombing for nothing. We're here for a purpose. We're going to do what we need to do, and then, I'm going to take you somewhere nice. I'm thinking the Cayman Islands. We haven't been there yet, and you always said that you wanted to go there. Right?"

I nodded.

"Alright then. Let's do what we came here to do, and then we'll disappear. Just me and you, baby. Like always. You know I don't want nobody but you," Kemp lied.

Yeah…right.

I knew from the moment he told me he'd started sleeping with Lava there was something special about her.

Kemp wasn't an easy man to impress.

He was so smart and calculated.

So observant, focused, and guarded.

He didn't have friends. An associate or two here and there but the only friend he had, in the whole wide world, was me. Whether it was by default or by choice—who knows. But I did know he wasn't exactly a "people person". Never had been. Never would be.

Yet, somehow, Lava had managed to break through his barriers. She'd managed to get Kemp to let her in. To let her into his space, his bed, and his head. And most importantly, his heart.

Kemp pulled me close to him and, though he was talking, I was so consumed with my thoughts I didn't hear anything he'd said.

My husband loves me.

Of course, he does.

But I also knew that although she was out of sight, Lava wasn't out of his mind.

She was the only other woman that he'd ever touched. No matter what I did or had to do, he'd always remained faithful to me…until she came along.

He'd been approached by all types of women.

Why wouldn't he be?

He was absolutely gorgeous. If men could be called such a thing. But he never let that get to his head. He never gave another woman the time of day. He never gave them his attention.

But he'd given it to her.

It had to be something about her. And whether Lava knew it or not, she had stolen a piece of my husband that belonged to me. All I wanted was for her to *give him back* to me…completely.

It had been quite some time since the bombing. And since I'd faked my death and had the baby.

Now we were back in the U.S. and we had another task at hand.

We were here to ruin a few lives—again.

We had to pull some major strings and pay off more people than I could keep up with, but Kemp was no longer being called a terrorist. He was no longer the bombing suspect. In fact, although he was guilty of the crime, the rest of the world now believed it was someone else.

Thompson, the man that took the blame for the bombing, was paid handsomely and would never see the inside of a prison. Once the *show* of a trial was over, he would be transported to another country. He would live out the rest of his life wealthy and in peace, promising to never return to the United States again.

It wasn't all that hard to pull off, especially since Thompson was at the courthouse that day. He was there to beg his wife *not* to file for divorce. Funny thing was, she was the one having an affair, but he wanted them to stay together. He wanted them to work it out, but she refused. She was in love with someone else. Long story short, after begging her to no avail, he left her inside, walking out of the courthouse only two minutes before Kemp and before the bomb went off.

His wife died that day.

He'd just been standing there on the sidewalk as though he was waiting for someone or a ride. Once the bomb went off, everyone was seen running and screaming in a panic; everyone except for him.

On the camera footage we'd accessed from the administrative building across the street, we zoomed in to see Thompson standing there with a huge smile on his face.

He appeared to be happy, hopeful that his adulterous wife was dead.

He got his wish.

And then Kemp got an idea. He was so good at reading people. That was one of his many talents. And just from the way that Thompson put his hands in his pockets with his head high and walked away from the scene, knowing his wife was probably inside of the building hurt or dead, Kemp knew he could be convinced to do the unthinkable. Kemp said that for the right amount of money and a few guarantees Thompson could be convinced to take the blame for the bombing.

And he was right.

He did.

Thompson took the blame and turned himself in.

He told the police he'd bombed the courthouse to kill his wife. He urged them to look at his reaction from the footage that day as Kemp instructed him.

Though there were a few doubts, they couldn't deny his confession or that he was at the scene of the crime at the exact time. Still, there were a few questions. Some still believed that Kemp was an accomplice, so we had to do a few more pay-offs to turn all heads towards Thompson and all eyes off Kemp.

And just like that, Kemp was in the clear.

Neither Kemp nor I could believe he'd made a mistake that day at the courthouse. We'd had plenty of time and connections, so he knew the layout of the courthouse like the back of his hand. He knew where every single camera was, and with the two officers that were working that day to make sure he got inside without a problem, everything should've gone smoothly. Everything should've gone according to plan.

But it hadn't.

Kemp was always so careful, but he'd said that he'd gotten distracted for only a second and walked right in front of a camera.

If you asked me, it was because of his dealings with Lava. Lava had taken him off his game. Had she never come in the picture, he wouldn't have been acting so…soft. He would've been spot on, and everything would have gone off without a hitch. There wouldn't have been any problems. He would've never made a mistake.

Luckily, we'd found a way out of it, no matter how much it had cost us.

But at least Kemp was free.

Of course, a face like Kemp's was hard to forget so, at times, he got a few stares from being posted all over the news for months. Other than that, everything had been fine since we'd been back.

For now.

We were about to make another mess, and hopefully, there wouldn't be any mistakes.

Kemp and I have been together for what seems like forever. He was only fifteen when we got married. I was eighteen. Our marriage was arranged, and we met for the very first time on our wedding day back in Egypt.

Though Kemp was younger than I was, it was my father who made our marriage happen.

I never questioned why he'd chosen Kemp for me. I was sure he would've picked someone else. Someone who was on our level…financially. But instead, Kemp, a boy whom I'd never so much as seen around before, was the face I saw once he lifted my veil.

After taking our vows, life moved extremely fast for us but somewhere along the way, somehow, we still managed to fall in love. For the most part, all we had was each other. And as our love grew for each other over the years, the more it was tested; especially once we joined my father's organization.

My father was the wealthiest man in Cairo, and one of the wealthiest in the world. He was also one of the most dangerous. He was involved with an organization that fought for equality for our people, but that was his cover-up. Though the organization was all about peaceful resolutions, my father had his own agenda.

My father, Zee, as most people called him, liked to take matters into his own hands and solve things in his own way. He liked money and he enjoyed power, but he *loved* having people in his back pocket to use at his expense.

In my opinion, he wanted to rule the world.

And he was almost there. He had endless connections. Powerful ones, political ones, all over the world that he'd either paid, bribed, or manipulated into business arrangements with him over the years. I learned at a very young age that people would do just about anything for money. And with more than enough of it, my father developed a team of people who gets shit done at all costs. All he had to do was ask.

In his defense, and believe it or not, sometimes, he actually managed to make a difference. When he wasn't making a mess or cleaning up one.

That's where Kemp and I came in.

We were something like my father's employees…a part of his big, twisted, disastrous crew.

I wouldn't say we were terrorists, though some of our actions might've seemed that way. The label, to me, wasn't exactly accurate. My father actually didn't have a problem with America, and he often made it clear that not everyone in the States were an enemy. In fact, some of his most powerful allies were here.

Terrorists was definitely the wrong word.

Everything we did had a purpose.

It was for a reason.

And because of the things we did, different doors had opened for changes to be made; here and back *home*.

Some of the public figures and threats we'd destroyed or gotten rid of saved tons of lives in the process. Whether the world knew it or not, our actions helped save millions. It may not have produced immediate results but with time it proved to be a necessary evil. Then some of the things we'd done were simply to have someone in place to keep my father informed, more powerful and wealthier than he already was. But for the most part, we made the world a better place; even if our way of doing so was a bit impractical.

And in return, we lived well.

There was nothing Kemp and I wanted that we couldn't have. There was nothing we couldn't do. No place we couldn't go. Not to mention, we actually believed in the cause.

Well, at least at first.

Kemp and I worked for my father, but we hadn't known how sticky things could become in the beginning. We hadn't known the truth about the things we would have to do. And if I was being honest, killing people had taken some getting used to.

We told ourselves it was for the greater good, but I wasn't sure if either of us still believed it.

For example, the courthouse bombing was only to kill two crooked federal judges that were inside of it. They were involved in human trafficking and they had positions my father said he *needed*.

They were scheduled to be there at the same time, on the same day, and both had to be taken out. They were Kemp's targets. The bombing was for them, but innocent people died as well.

They were just collateral damage.

It's a sad, cold, horrible truth, but that's all that it was.

I personally thought the bombing was a bit extreme. Usually, if someone had to die, everything was discreetly handled. However, the bombing was a direct order from my father and he said it was necessary. The men he wanted to replace the deceased judges needed to look like they deserved the positions. There needed to be chaos and they needed to look heroic. And they did. They'd been waiting for the bomb to go off that day. Once it did, they were all over the news with the firefighters and police, helping get people to safety. A few reporters that worked for my father were also on the scene to ensure they captured shots of the desired successors carrying some of the victims.

My father got exactly what he wanted.

As for Kemp…he had killed two men who were selling women and children for their own financial gain.

That was the light in all the darkness.

I guess.

The thing is, the lies we told ourselves about the things we did were no longer working.

Some might ask why was I still so loyalty to my father, his plans, and the movement after all this time?

My answer was simple.

I was supposed to be. I'd been raised to be.

And I was sure that Kemp had a few reasons of his own.

In our younger years and the beginning years of marriage, we'd received some of the best training in the world. We'd been taught everything from self-defense, foreign languages, advanced technology education, and psychological training. We'd even been taught how to kill someone with our bare hands.

We'd been groomed to do the things that we did, and after a while, we simply got used to doing them.

My role is usually simple, though sometimes they involved sex with other men in order to gain their trust and get secrets and information from them.

Kemp's roles are usually a little more hands-on.

He is a protector.

And…a killer.

He cleaned up the mess and took care of the dirty work. If someone had to pull the trigger, it was usually him. Whether it was someone that was in the way or someone my father deemed to be a problem, Kemp was his go-to person to handle it.

He was efficient, effective, and everything he did was usually well thought out and on purpose.

Except for her.

Kemp would never admit it, but if you ask me, I think he loves her.

Lava.

Usually, though he knew I had to have sex with other men, Kemp never bothered to entertain other women. He always kept to himself, played his part, and then he would remind me I was his by screwing me good and hard every chance he could.

Sometimes, I would deal with other men for months, even a year at a time, but he always said he knew I was only doing what I had to do. He swore he didn't have any interest in being involved with another woman.

How did Lava change his mind?

How did she get him to break his rule?

Maybe it was because I'd gotten pregnant by another man. I never meant to hurt him that way.

For the most part, when other men touched me, I imagined they were Kemp. That was the only way to get through it. Well, that and having a drink or two.

That night, the only night I could've gotten pregnant by George, Lava's husband's best friend, he'd invited me to a hotel room. I took the opportunity to get him drunk so that I could ask questions about his wife and her political family, but somewhere along the way, I ended up drinking more than I should have. I was off my game. I was drunk. And I'd forgotten to make him use protection.

I always used protection.

Even with my husband.

I had horrible side effects to birth control, so I was always careful. I'd never made a mistake. *Until that night.*

Nevertheless, I ended up pregnant.

It hurt Kemp to the core. Telling him was the hardest thing I ever had to do. Telling him that I was keeping it and that I just couldn't get an abortion was the second.

Ironically, though I was involved with all kinds of horrible, unforgivable things, I just couldn't kill the baby growing inside me.

And though Kemp was furious and wanted me to get rid of it, he respected my wishes and allowed me to carry another man's child.

Maybe that's why he slept with her.

No, that couldn't be the reason. At least, not at first because now that I think about it I think he'd slept with her before I found out the baby news.

So initially, it was something else.

Maybe it was just something he felt with her.

Something he had yet to feel with me.

I knew he wouldn't leave me though.

We loved each other, we understood each other. We were attached. We were connected. And we didn't believe in divorce.

But that night, when he told me he'd had sex with Lava for the very first time, the shame in his eyes told me that even he couldn't control his feelings and urges for her. I knew he'd thought long and hard, probably for days or weeks, before actually crossing that line with her. That's just how he was. I also knew that since he'd done it, since he'd had screwed her, it was because he'd wanted to.

Though I'd been with other men, it was never because I'd wanted to do it. And he knew that. I couldn't believe that he'd stepped out on me, willingly.

I was hurt, but I figured it was a one-time thing.

It wasn't.

It happened again, and again, and again.

And he always told me.

At the time, being that I was pregnant by George, I felt like I couldn't say much of anything, especially since he'd begged me to terminate the pregnancy. Every time he told me he'd made another mistake by sleeping with her, I thought maybe I deserved it.

I remembered seeing her coming out of the bar our organization owns back in Fairfax. I wanted to grab her by the throat and strangle her. It had taken everything in me to put a smile on my face that day and pretend I didn't know she was fucking my husband.

Finally, I knew how it felt to be in his shoes. Watching me, knowing I was sleeping with other men.

I knew how it felt to be all the women whose husbands' I'd had sex with. And I knew how it felt to be her…Lava.

Knowing we would be leaving soon, I told myself she didn't mean anything to him.

I was wrong.

She'd meant something. But he was just going to have to get over it. I wasn't pregnant anymore, so I no longer felt guilty. And I would never let my husband go without a fight.

"Kiss me," Kemp said, interrupting my thoughts and reminding me he was there.

We were in Washington D.C. and pretending to be siblings again.

I was there to cause a scandal with someone in a high, respectable position as an employee for the government. I was going to have an affair with him, leak it, and ruin his marriage and career.

Kemp was there to look after me and…to kill him--- our next target. And then someone on my father's payroll was going to take his position.

I hadn't had sex with anyone else in a while, and I wondered if he would still view it as "work" or if he would see it as an opening to do his own thing again.

Surprisingly, more than anything else, that was my biggest concern.

I kissed his awaiting lips.

"You ready?" he asked.

"Always."

Kemp walked out the door and told me that he would be back later.

We'd moved into the same apartment complex but in two separate buildings; right across the parking lot from each other.

Of course, we couldn't live in the same place once the affair started.

I'd studied our next target, my new victim, Dedrick Harden, for a few weeks, and it was finally time to get this show on the road. I had a few months to work my magic and get close to him. Hopefully, it wouldn't take long for him to fall for me.

After that, it would be easy-peasy.

Once I had pictures, videos, and whatever else we would need, we would cause a big mess. We had a journalist in town, waiting to report the affair and plaster pictures in the newspaper. His life, his marriage, and his reputation would all go up in flames. Then he would end up dead. Kemp said he was going to make it look like a suicide. I'd asked him why Dedrick had to die in the first place when we were already destroying his image. I was sure the scandal would force him resign and then my father could still have what he wanted. I liked that idea better.

Killing him just seemed so extreme.

And I was tired of people dying.

Not every man I'd been with ended up dead. Only a few. Usually, Kemp would be in the same city just to watch me or take care of other people and problems that didn't have anything to do with my task. But this was one of the times he was involved. All he knew was my father wanted him dead at the end of it all, which meant there was probably a reason or something else that Dedrick was involved in I didn't know about yet.

I stepped over the boxes and walked towards the mirror hanging on the wall.

I'd dyed and cut my hair for the first time ever.

I'd always loved my long, dark, beautiful hair. It was my glory. And in a way, it was my strength.

But for now, it was gone.

Currently, my hair was short, curly, and copper red. And unexpectedly, I kind of liked it.

I hadn't been in an extremely bad light, not like Kemp had been, but there was some media coverage on my fake death, especially once the questions about the bombing and Kemp started coming into play since I was his "sister" and all.

And since I'd had my share of interactions with men who were either wealthy, affiliated with the government or had a few connections that were deemed important, changing my hair and wearing hazel contacts was an attempt to switch up my appearance.

I was still very, very beautiful as I'd always been but other than my tinted skin, my Egyptian roots were questionable, almost invisible. I doubted anyone from the past would recognize me at first glance. Though, once Dedrick's affair hit the fan, I was sure the men I'd been with would realize it was me but by then, the damage would already be done, and I would be long gone.

Most—well, all the men I'd been with had somehow fallen in love with me. Some of them a lot more than others. As bad as it sounded, I'd been taught well, and I was good at my "job".

I was just hoping there was some way Dedrick wouldn't have to die. I didn't want anyone else to die because of me.

Unless it was Lava.

She wasn't going to take my Kemp away from me.

Grabbing my laptop, I took a seat on the couch.

My thoughts of Lava had caused me to think about someone else.

Tokyo.

After typing in the fake name Tokyo was going by on social media, I started to go through her pictures.

Of course, Kemp told me why he'd given the baby to Tokyo instead of to George. I couldn't say I wanted the baby back because I didn't. But sometimes he would cross my mind, so I would look at the pictures she had of him online.

It hadn't taken Kemp long to find Tokyo's fake name and all her social media accounts. There was nothing he couldn't find or do. Nothing he couldn't fix. And he could hack anything.

I was sure she wasn't using her real name because of all the mess she'd caused. I clicked on her page and, immediately, I smiled.

The baby was getting so big.

I stared at the pictures of him and Tokyo together.

She looked so happy and so did he.

As I went through the photos, I wondered why Lava's sister had stopped being in them.

I, for one, was shocked when Kemp told me he'd caught her and Tokyo in a hotel room. I was more shocked when he told me why Tokyo was sleeping with Lava's husband in the first place.

Lava had no idea she'd been to blame for her own mess. Had she never fooled around with her sister's husband, Tokyo wouldn't have been messing around with hers.

And Lava's sister was…

I'm not even sure what to say about her. I was definitely not the one to judge but to go to the extreme she had just to get back at Lava…

Savage!

Looking at dates on the photos, it had been months since Lava's sister was in one.

Maybe she left…

Maybe she'd gone back home to her family in Virginia.

I smiled as I watched a video of the baby wobbling towards Tokyo. She'd named him Japan.

She made a horrible friend and an even worse mistress, but she seemed to be a damn good mother.

A better mother than I could've ever been.

For Kemp and I, kids had never been in our plans.

Not after we'd committed ourselves to doing the things we did. But lately, I wondered if we'd done enough. I wondered what life would be like if we decided to do things differently.

If we decided to be…normal.

Kemp didn't know it yet, but I'd already talked to my father about us getting out. After this job was over, my father agreed it was time for us to enjoy our lives.

It was no secret I was my father's only weakness. Not my mother, his wife of over thirty years or any of his other possessions, but me. I'd always known all I had to do was ask, and he would give me his blessing to stop and be happy. I guess it was just all I knew for so long I wasn't sure what would come after it.

But observing the baby again, I was ready.

I was ready to start a new life with my husband. I hadn't talked to Kemp about it, but I was going to. Hopefully, he felt the same way. Who knows, maybe then we could try for a baby of our own. It was worth a shot.

Either way, it was time for us to live in peace.

It was time for us to be…free.

~***~

KEMP

I watched Satin from a distance.

It was late evening and she was attending an event where she was hoping to run into Dedrick, her next fool.

All eyes were going to be on her.

Every man in the room would be staring at her, and he would be no different.

My wife was fine as hell.

Always had been. Always would be.

Satin wore a fitted, knee-length black dress, and her reddish-orange looking hair really brought out her fake hazel eyes. The name she was using tonight was fake too. Along with her fake journalist credentials. She was supposedly there to cover the party but her only concern and focus would be getting next to him.

Once she disappeared through the double doors, I drove away.

Speeding, I was convinced this was the last time. After this job, me and my wife were done.

I hadn't mentioned it to Satin yet, but shit, I got the feeling we were on the same page. The bombing had been a close call. Even before then, I'd had the feeling it was time for us to bring things to the end.

From the beginning, I knew what I was signing up to do by marrying her. I knew what I was signing up to become. Zee, her father, or Pops as I called him, told me he needed me. He needed me to work for him. He needed to be able to trust me. Marrying his daughter was something like an incentive. I'd always known.

I came from nothing.

My family was poor and barely making it from one day to the next before the marriage.

My father was a good man and he worked hard, but it wasn't enough. Year after year, no matter what he tried to do to take care of us, he always seemed to fail. My mother's side of the family didn't have much of anything either.

And then one day many years ago my father was approached by a rich man, saying I would make the perfect husband for his daughter. When he told him, my family would become wealthy, my father agreed.

I married Satin, and my family's life changed forever.

Now, everyone was happy.

Except for me.

I wasn't sure I knew what happiness was.

I'd spent almost twenty years paying my dues to Satin's father for rescuing my family from poverty.

After the initial request, I met with him days before the wedding, alone, and he told me about his organization. He also told me about what he did in the shadows. At the time, I didn't have a problem joining the movement or working with him. Restoring peace and justice. I didn't mind coming over here destroying people at first because I wasn't too fond of this country.

I'd lied to Lava.

I really was Egyptian and black, but my mother wasn't exactly the cause of it. She was only half of a beautiful black queen. My grandmother, her mother, had fallen in love with an American soldier; a black man and had an affair.

It ruined her life.

After she gave birth to my mother, her husband and the man I called my grandfather, made her life pure hell until the day she died. My mother was five. From that point on, the man that raised my mother groomed her to hate Americans. He told her that an American black soldier raped her mother, ruining their lives and marriage. I'd also been taught the same hate, though I blamed it all on Satin when telling Lava what I wanted her to believe.

It wasn't until a few years ago, on his death bed, that he told my mother the truth.

Had I known the truth a long time ago, maybe I would've tried to cut ties with Satin's father sooner. Especially once I realized that peace or justice had nothing to do with what Satin's father wanted.

Power. Money. Greed.

That's what it was all about.

In my defense, the people I was usually told to kill were bad people. Other than the innocent ones that were caught in the crossfire from time to time, the big fish, the targets, were usually powerful with dark and sometimes deadly secrets. They were either tied up in some shady ass business, traitors, murders, or worse.

But who was I to judge?

I was no angel my-damn-self.

However, my *do-boy* days were coming to an end.

After this *job*, I was done.

I wasn't sure how Pops was going to take it, but he had a soft spot for Satin so if I could get her onboard there was no doubt in my mind we couldn't get out.

Dedrick was my last hit.

And my wife's last…

Every story comes to an end.

This chapter that includes Pops, killing, and letting other men touch my wife was over.

And hopefully, Pops would see things my way, so I wouldn't have to kill him too.

I was my father-in-law's eyes and ears, his finger on a trigger, and usually the last person to see his targets or enemies alive.

He trusted me.

He trusted me with his life. With his daughter. With his money. With everything. It was going to be hard for him to let me go, but he didn't have a choice.

I'd paid my dues.

Now I wanted to be something more.

When I thought about forever, I saw Satin, me, and...sometimes Lava's unforgettable ass would show up in my thoughts.

In the back of my mind, she was always there.

I'd helped her get her life back on track with her husband, but that didn't mean I'd forgotten about her.

How could I?

After all, she reminded me of the first woman I ever fell in love with. I knew that was why I was so drawn to her.

I'd told Lava I'd never loved anyone but Satin, but that was a lie too. Before Satin and the arranged marriage, there was a beautiful woman named Rie.

And I loved her.

She was years older than I was, but at the time, I was sure she would end up being my wife.

As strange as it may sound, Lava reminded me so much of her. Though Rie was Egyptian, every time I looked at Lava's face I saw hers. Their face was the exact same shape. Lava, of course, was shapelier but if her and Rie were standing side by side and had the same shade of skin, you could easily mistake them for sisters, maybe even twins. They had the same hypnotic eyes. And every time I looked into Lava's eyes, I remembered all the moments I'd shared with Rie. The laughs and the secrets. The moments we'd stolen underneath the evening sun.

It's wild but they even had the same laugh.

I swear to God they did.

In a twisted way, being with Lava was like a chance at finally having the woman I'd wanted more than anything in the world at one point in time.

A chance at having the woman I never got to have.

That's what drew me to her.

When I looked at Lava, it was as though I was looking into the eyes of my true first love.

Though I never mentioned that part to Satin.

Lava's personality was just the icing on the cake. It kept me wanting to know more. There'd been something warm about her. Something comfortable from the very beginning. Something that reminded me I was human again.

Now, don't get me wrong, I love my wife.

Satin is my queen, and I would die protecting her. There's nothing in this world I wouldn't do for her. And I do mean nothing.

But Lava and I connected on a different level. One that was new to me. I liked the way I would feel whenever I was talking to or around her.

I was a person.

Not just someone's long term investment.

The sun disappeared as I drove, and it wasn't until Satin texted me that I glanced at the clock, realizing I'd been driving around in circles just thinking for a little over an hour and a half.

She told me she had linked with a few reporters and would be meeting them at a bar after she stopped by her apartment to change. I told her to go easy on the alcohol and to call a cab when she was done. I then texted Sheriff Rollyson. He worked for us…well, for Pops. I told him I had something to handle and gave him the name of the bar Satin told me she was going to. I instructed him to make it his business to go to the bar and keep an eye on Satin until I got back.

I had somewhere else to be.

I'd made up my mind I was hitting the road.

I needed to see her.

I was going to see Lava.

Fairfax, Virginia was about thirty-minutes away from where we were in Washington. I could get there and back before Satin even noticed.

Maybe if I saw her I could get her off my mind.

When Satin and I briefly dropped into the States a while ago, we were in North Carolina. I was only in town to handle some payoffs. I hadn't had time to check in on Lava then but now I had plenty of time.

I knew I was going to have to hear Satin's mouth about this because when she asked me where I'd been I was going to tell her the truth.

I tried my best not to lie to her unless I had to.

I told her almost everything. She was the only person in the world I could truly trust. I remembered telling her I'd had sex with Lava the first time. I left Lava asleep in my bed and went to Satin, just to tell her what I'd done.

I hadn't planned to fuck Lava, but I couldn't help myself. I'd wanted her. I'd wanted her more than anything else in the world at that moment. I just had to have her. And that surprised me.

Since marrying Satin, another woman could barely catch my attention, let alone keep it. I had a wife who was probably the most attractive woman I'd ever seen. Physically, she was a hell of a lot to compare to.

But Lava's familiar face, her smile, her laugh, and the depth of the conversations we'd shared seemed to have a bigger effect on me than I thought they would. Then I even realized at the time.

I just needed to lay my eyes on her.

Just one last time.

~***~

SATIN

"Welcome, Sandra Burkes," the lady said.

I'd almost forgotten she was talking to me.

I was using another fake name to attend a meeting.

Satin wasn't my real name either.

Nor was Kemp my husband's birth name, but they were the names we used the most. Hell, they were the names we'd grown accustom to calling each other instead of Mandisa, which was my real name and Nephi, which was Kemp's. These days, it was just easier for us to go by Kemp and Satin, so we did.

Honestly, I couldn't wait until I could just be Mandisa again.

No more Satin. No more Sandra.

Just me.

Kemp had gone to Virginia the other night.

We hadn't talked much about it but at the end of the day, really, what else was there to say?

He told me he wouldn't go and see her, but he'd gone anyway. It just confirmed what I already knew.

He'd done something we swore we would never do.

He'd fallen in love with someone else.

The lady led me towards Dedrick's wife's office.

At the party the other night, he'd barely even noticed me, so I figured I could pay his wife a little visit.

His wife, Carla, was some hotshot lawyer and since I was pretending to be this new, hungry for success journalist, I pretended to be interested in writing a piece on her and some of the recent cases she'd won.

A perfect cover and excuse to pry.

I planned on throwing in a few questions about Dedrick and, hopefully, she would give me something I could use. Something to speed up the process of making her husband fall for me.

The sooner I gave my father what he wanted, the sooner I could take my husband and put thousands of miles between him and his unforgettable mistress.

But first, I had to become one. *Again.*

My father not only wanted Dedrick's position within Homeland Security, but Kemp told me the other day Dedrick was also had ties to some huge drug operation. He was playing on both sides of the law. Kemp wouldn't say for sure but, if I had to guess, Dedrick's death was probably a favor from my father to one of his alliances. Probably someone who wanted Dedrick out the way in the drug world. I was almost sure of it.

I didn't see why I just couldn't stay out the way.

I didn't understand why the affair was even necessary this time around. With all the other men, the ones who died and the many that were still alive, I'd been sleeping with them to get something from them or out of them. Secrets, names, dirt…anything my father could use to his benefit. But with Dedrick, that wasn't the case.

There was nothing to gain. I just had to make him want me, have an affair, and ruin his good name.

Why not just skip to the end?

When I mentioned my thoughts to Kemp, all he said was my father wanted things done his way.

He wanted to tarnish Dedrick's name, completely tear his world apart, then kill him after making him suffer.

Pure evil.

Taking a deep breath, I walked inside Dedrick's wife's office. Carla noticeably did a double take once she saw me.

I'm pretty sure she was taken back by my beauty.

Everyone always was.

Finally, she stood up with a smile.

"Good morning, I'm Mrs. Harden." She extended her hand.

Smiling back, I shook her hand and observed her.

She was tall, especially wearing heels, but she was cute. She was in her early forties, light-skinned, and she had short black hair. She was slim and the best feature on her face were her lips.

"It's an honor to be sitting down with you," I said to her once I took a seat. "I don't want to take up too much of your time so let's get started."

I asked her a few random questions.

She didn't hesitate to answer them and, as she talked and talked, I pretended to listen.

Keeping a smile on my face, I shifted my thoughts to Lava.

For some reason, that day at her job came to my mind.

I'd applied for the position with her company on purpose.

I'd known who she and her husband were from the very beginning because I always researched our targets. Since I was there to get close to George, just as a precaution, I took a glance at close friends and family. I like to be thorough. Anyway, during that whole process, I came across his best friend, West, and while I was at it I remembered briefly checking into Lava.

I'd been seeing and sleeping with George for months, trying to find dirt on his wife's political family. They seemed as clean as a whistle, but my father was convinced there was something to be found. He said everyone had a secret. Something they don't want anyone to know, and he wanted me to find out what it was. But after months into it and barely getting anywhere I wanted to try another possible source.

Lava.

I'd seen the job opening on the company's website and applied. I was hoping to get the job and maybe get a little information out of her since George mentioned she and his wife were pretty good friends as well. I figured if we worked together something useful would come out during a little girl talk or something.

I was sure I was going to get the job. My résumé was perfect. But at the time, I hadn't known she thought I was her husband's mistress. I hadn't known West had lied to her and said he was having an affair with me.

His lie messed up everything.

Not to mention that his lie almost got me killed!

I really did have an allergic reaction, thanks to Lava, that night at the bar. Thankfully, Kemp was on the scene and knew exactly what to do. A doctor on my father's payroll met us at the hospital. It was Kemp's idea to have the doctor report I'd died since he was about to bomb the courthouse and we were going to disappear anyway.

Carla laughed, pulling me away from my flashback and causing me to give her my attention.

I asked her a few more questions about her work then I threw in a few about Dedrick, but nothing that she said was useful.

Once the interview was over, she thanked me, and her assistant showed me to the door. Outside, just as I was about to drive away, I noticed Dedrick getting out of a car that had pulled in front of the building.

He looked behind him in my direction, but I turned my head as I drove past him.

I stared at him in my rearview mirror, looking like a tall glass of chocolate milk until he disappeared.

I'll get him.

Trust me.

I always do.

****

Chapter Two

KEMP

"Hey, can I talk to you about something?" Satin asked.

"You can talk to this dick," I answered.

Satin rolled her eyes and stuck up her middle finger.

I grinned at her.

I was wearing her down.

Satin had been mad at me for the past few days, but I couldn't blame her.

I'd gone to Virginia just to sit across the street from Lava's house all night long. I saw her the next morning, but I didn't speak to her. She didn't even know I was there. I just watched her.

She came out her house with the kids, looking as beautiful as ever. She was smiling.

Happy.

After loading all five of the kids into her new jeep, she drove away.

The last time I spoke to her she told me she was pregnant, but I didn't see a baby. Being that West left out before she did, I was sure the baby wasn't inside.

I wondered what happened.

"I need to talk to you about something for real, stupid," Satin growled, demanding my attention.

I picked up her feet and placed them into my lap once she sat down on the couch beside of me.

"I'm listening."

"So...Well..." she started. "I was thinking..."

"Damn, say it already!"

She grunted. "After this *job*...I'm done," she blurted.

I paused.

"I'm tired, Kemp. We've been doing all this for way too long, basically our whole lives, and I'm tired. I want to be normal. I want to do normal things. Like normal people. And I already told my father."

Oh shit.

I was his investment, so I had a feeling he wouldn't want to let me go too easily.

"And he said okay. After this, we are free. Once we do whatever we have to do with Dedrick, we're done, Kemp. No more of all this. What do you say?"

I moved her feet and pulled her closer to me.

"Damn. You want to know what's funny? I've been feeling the exact same way for a very long time," I told her.

"Really?"

"Really."

She beamed. "And with me? Do you want to be normal and spend the rest of your life being happy with me?" she asked.

I stroked her bottom lip with my thumb.

"Come on now. Who else would I want to spend it with?"

She stared at me, as though she wanted to ask about Lava, but she didn't. But I could read her. I knew her, so I kissed her to confirm my words for her.

I really did mean them.

A life without Satin wasn't an option. I would never leave her. I just had to get my mind right.

That's all.

"I love you."

"Not as much as I love you."

Satin positioned herself on top of me.

I kissed her again, starting with her lips then made my way down to her neck. She pulled back and took off her tank top, exposing her nipples. I didn't hesitate to place her left breast in my mouth.

The more she cooed, the harder my dick became.

And once she started to gyrate her hips, I slightly lifted her from my lap and ripped her panties at the sides.

She giggled.

Naked, I laid her on her back and opened her legs.

Impatiently, she waited for me to taste her, but I wanted her to beg for it. She bit her bottom lip, and I smiled at her. She started to breath heavily, but still, I waited. Finally, she begged me to please her, so I did.

I tasted her, teased her, and satisfied her most prized possession with my tongue. Her moans aroused me, motivated me to work harder. She already knew I wasn't coming up for air until she was cuming in my mouth.

And it didn't take her long.

After a few short minutes, Satin exhaled contently, but she knew we were just getting started. It was late night, we were at my apartment and I was only wearing boxers and gym shorts. Without feeling like messing up the mood to find a condom, I promised Satin I would pull out. She opened her legs wide, inviting me inside of them.

Once in position, I stroked her pleasantly as I stared deeply into her eyes.

Sex with Satin had always been just what I needed it to be. She would do anything to please me, and she allowed me to do anything to her with no complaints and no questions asked.

I came in close, so close I could smell the scent of the lavender body wash on her skin. My lips found their way to hers and, without letting up while stroking to my own steady beat, I kissed her like I'd never kissed her before. I kissed her from my soul. I kissed her from my heart.

She might not have been my first love, or even the woman I would've chosen had the decision been mine, but she was the one I had been given. The one I never wanted to lose or live without.

Satin pulled her lips away from mine.

"Baby, baby," she moaned. "Come on. Tear this pussy up."

Yeah.

That's just what I like to hear.

Our bodies separated but my dick stayed deep inside her as I went to work. Pound after pound, I tortured her pussy, and she took her *punishment* like a pro.

Finally, her body stiffened beneath me and she started to curse. Knowing I had to get mine while she was getting hers, with one last pump, I pulled out just as my dick *spit up* on her thighs.

Breathing heavy, I collapsed onto the floor. She rolled off the couch and into my arms.

"I love you, baby," she whispered.

I smirked as I looked over at her.

"I love you too, La—baby."

I corrected myself but not fast enough.

Satin sat up in a hurry, screaming as she hit me with her tiny fists over and over again.

All I could do was try to explain.

Why in the fuck had I almost called her Lava's name?

~***~

SATIN

"Are you in line?" Dedrick asked behind me.

I'd followed him to a store.

I was hanging around near the counter as though I was looking for something else to buy.

I wasn't.

I'd just been waiting for him to notice me.

I looked at him with a smile.

"Sorry. You can go ahead."

He eyed me hungrily as though I was a big juicy steak he wanted to devour and then suck on the bones.

"It's you," he said to my surprise. "I saw you not too long ago. At a party, I believe. I remember because you were the prettiest woman in the room, and you had every available bachelor drooling in your face," he smiled.

"Oh, yeah. You look familiar too. And I think I know what party you are referring to. I'm a journalist. I'm new at it so I was just getting my feet wet. And since you weren't a part of the drooling, that can only mean one thing…you're unavailable." I smirked.

Dedrick chuckled.

He stepped up to pay for the drink that was in his hand.

I couldn't help but to stare at him.

He was middle-aged, tall, and handsome.

He wore a low fade and the few gray hairs in his beard seemed to stand out against his black coffee, no crème skin. He wore an expensive Italian suit, and he had the most charismatic smile I'd ever seen.

He was attractive. Not *Kemp* attractive, but he was definitely the most attractive of the men I'd played with over the years.

And speaking of Kemp, I was so pissed at him!

Since he'd almost called me Lava the other night after making love to me, I was convinced my marriage would never be the same.

I'd lost a part of him.

And I wasn't sure I would ever get it back.

Unless I got rid of the problem.

And Lava, whether she knew it or not, was one big ass problem!

Now, more than ever, I was desperate to ruin Dedrick's life, so I could try and salvage what was left of mine.

Dedrick stood there for a while, as though he was waiting for something.

"Have you found what you were looking for yet?"

"Excuse me?" I asked.

"I know you don't think I'm going to let you pay for your own things, do you?"

He smiled. I blushed.

I placed my items on the counter. Once he paid for them, he handed them to me and walked with me towards the door.

He smelled so good I accidently closed my eyes as I inhaled the scent of his skin.

"Thank you." I smiled at him.

"You are more than welcome."

He stopped in front of a car that was waiting for him.

Slowly, I started to walk away. I placed one foot in front of the other, swaying my hips from side to side as I walked, knowing that he was watching me.

How could he not be?

"Wait." I finally heard him say.

I stopped, but I didn't turn around.

"You're right, I am unavailable. But what if I was drooling?" he asked.

I smiled.

After removing the smirk from my face, I turned around to face him.

Gotcha.

~***~

"Baby, can we make up now? Please."

"Kemp, fuck you."

He laughed, but I mugged him, so he hurriedly clamped his mouth shut.

I couldn't be sure when I would get over it all, but I was sure it wouldn't be anytime soon. It had been almost two weeks and I was still hotter than a summer day in Texas, at the end of June about what he'd said.

Before sex, during sex, and after sex, no-goddamn-body was supposed to be on his mind but me! Besides, I was sure Kemp just wanted to make up because he wanted some. He was acting like he was going to croak over and die if I didn't let him touch me, and I was enjoying watching him whine and complain.

Kemp grumbled for a little while longer, and then he changed the subject. "Have you and Dedrick…"

"No, I'm still in the *playing hard to get* stage," I confirmed.

That day at the store, I'd lightly flirted with him then pointed at the ring on his finger and told him I didn't sleep with married men.

I proceeded to fill his head with compliments and endless possibilities of things we could've gotten into if he hadn't been married.

Then I walked away from him, knowing the next time I saw him I would be singing a different tune.

When Dedrick and I crossed paths again, I would crank the flirting up a notch. I would tell him all the things a man wanted and needed to hear. Him being married would no longer be an issue. After that, the rest would pretty much be in the bag from there.

I could've ran into him again a long time ago, but I knew making him wonder about me, who I was, and where I was for a while would have his mind right where I wanted and needed it to be.

"Don't you think you should give me some? You know, before all of that?"

"Go get it from Lava," I huffed.

"Satin…"

"What? I mean you might as well. After all, you almost said you loved *her*."

"I love you. Period. Now, don't say that shit no more," Kemp growled.

"No, you—"

"What the fuck did I just say, huh? Satin, I love you. Not Lava. Okay?"

"Whatever."

Going back and forth with him was pointless.

"Can I at least have a kiss?" Kemp asked.

I stood up and walked towards his apartment door. "Sure. You can kiss my ass." Then I opened the door and slammed it behind me.

The breeze was cool as I hurried across the parking lot to my apartment building. Most nights I stayed at Kemp's for his peace of mind, but tonight, I just wanted to be alone.

The little old lady that lived next door to me came out her front door just as I passed by it. Her little dog barked, and I had to stop my foot from kicking the shit out of it.

I hate dogs.

Almost as much as I hate Lava.

I entered my apartment and rushed towards my computer after kicking off my shoes.

Lately, I'd been watching Lava's social media like a crazy person! I wanted to know what it was he saw in her that he didn't see in me.

I read through all her online posts and it pissed me off she seemed so happy while I felt like shit. Like I was still sharing my husband with her.

She made jokes about her husband and their kids and, from what I could see, Kemp was the last thing on her mind.

Then why is she still on his?

~***~

"So, you have to answer this question for me," Dedrick said.

After getting his schedule from our leak inside his office, I'd found out he had a business dinner.

I dressed in a sexy, skin tight, blazing red dress that made my booty look about three times bigger than it actually was. I slipped on a new pair of Louis Vuitton's, threw on some diamonds, and arrived at the restaurant thirty minutes before his scheduled business dinner.

When Dedrick walked in, I was already on my second drink and about to order my food.

Almost immediately after taking his seat, he noticed me, excused himself from his table, and headed in my direction.

Once he found out I was dining alone, he walked back over to his table, and shortly after, I saw his business date get up and leave.

Dedrick then asked if he could join me.

"What's your question?"

"How can someone as beautiful as you are not be married? Or taken? I'm just curious. What? Are you crazy or something? Yes, that has to be it." Dedrick chuckled.

"I had a husband. He died," I lied.

"Wow. I'm sorry to hear that."

"It's okay. It was a long time ago."

The waiter took his drink order.

"Anyway, after him, I've just been cautious about dating. I don't date much and I don't mind being alone. I don't mind dressing up and going out by myself. Obviously."

I smiled at him. "When it's my time again, the right man will come along and sweep me off my feet. I'm in no rush." I looked him directly in the eyes.

Dedrick fixed his tie.

We stared at each other in silence until the waiter came back to the table with my food in her hands.

"Well, I couldn't leave you to eat all by yourself," Dedrick said, seeing I didn't touch my fork, planning to wait until he was served.

The way he looked at me, I could tell he was trying to figure me out.

Maybe he was wondering how far he would get to go with me. Or if I even really wanted his company at all.

So, I helped him out.

"I am glad that you decided to join me. It's always nice to have someone to talk to." I touched his arm and, just from the way he cleared his throat, I knew his dick was probably rock hard. I also knew by the end of the night I would have him eating out the palm of my hand.

Let the games begin.

As the night went on, we discussed topic after topic and let's just say I was pleasantly surprised.

We talked and laughed and actually seemed to have a few things in common. He challenged me. He made me think about things I hadn't thought about in years. I found myself genuinely laughing at his jokes and a few of his compliments managed to make me feel all warm and fuzzy inside.

I don't know. It was like talking to him just felt…easy. I couldn't quite explain it.

And in a way, I didn't want the night to end.

We had dinner, a few more drinks, and then we just sat there enjoying each other's company. We were so lost in conversation we didn't notice we'd sat there chatting all night until it was time for the restaurant to close.

"Wow, I really enjoyed talking to you tonight," I said, which was nothing but the truth.

"Yeah. I haven't had a good conversation like that with anyone in quite some time," he said. "If ever. Maybe we should do it again."

I eyed him as though he was up to something. "I'm not sure your wife would like that," I said, knowing I was going to agree to seeing him again anyway.

"She wouldn't care. She only wants my time and my attention when it's convenient for her or for a credible mention that I'm her husband. I'm sure you've noticed she hasn't called me. Not even once." He paused. "Don't take what I'm saying the wrong way. I've never cheated on my wife before or even thought about it. But you…"

The way he looked at me sent a chill down my spine. It was filled with something I'd never seen before. It wasn't lust. It wasn't attraction. I'm not even sure what it was, but no one had ever looked at me like that before.

Not even my own husband.

In that moment, I wished I'd never agreed to do this to him. I wished he didn't have to die.

Most of the men I'd used on my father's behalf were still alive. There had only been two, soon-to-be three, I knew would end up dead from the very beginning.

And I wished there was some way it didn't have to happen to Dedrick.

"Okay."

"Okay what?"

"Maybe we can hang out again. Strictly *platonic*. After all, a man and a woman can just be friends, right?" I asked.

He nodded. "Right," he lied.

That day at the store, I'd given him my *other* fake name, Sandra. The same name I'd given to his wife.

Dedrick passed me his phone and I typed in that name and the number to the prepaid phone in my purse. I knew tonight was going to end here. I just hadn't expected to like him.

Dedrick asked if we could meet again for dinner at the end of the week and, after I agreed, he walked me to my car. Once I was inside, we hugged, said goodnight, and then he walked away.

I started my car and pretended as though I was preparing to drive away. Once Dedrick pulled off, I let out a deep breath and glanced in my rearview mirror at the car parked directly behind mine.

Kemp.

~***~

KEMP

I'd been waiting for her as always, making sure she was okay.

I was never too far away when she was doing her thing. If I couldn't be there, I always had someone else there in my place.

Watching.

I picked up my phone once her face popped up on the screen.

"We're going to dinner again at the end of the week."

"Good. The sooner the better. The sooner we can go," I said as we pulled out the parking lot and drove in the same direction.

I was tired of sharing her.

She belonged to me.

It was never easy sharing my wife with another man. I hadn't even known that would be the case. I felt like a fool for not putting a stop to it from the very beginning.

"He's already texting me."

"He a thirsty motherfucker, ain't he?"

She laughed.

"You going home?"

"Nah. I'm going to follow you there then I'm going to check on a few other things," I said.

"Virginia?" she asked.

"No."

We talked about random things and once she got out her car and walked into the apartment building I pulled off. I pulled out one of my other phones. It was normal for me to have two or three phones at a time.

I'd placed a tracker underneath Dedrick's car while they were inside the restaurant I opened the app on the phone, found his location, and headed towards it.

As I followed the navigation, I already knew that he hadn't gone home. I'd watched his house a few times before and when I noticed I was heading downtown I figured he was probably going to check on his other stream of revenue.

Drugs.

He didn't actually sell them or anything like that. No, he wasn't that type of man. From what Pops knew, he just made it a little easier for them to be moved around. Pulled a few strings here and there.

And apparently, he played favorites.

Pops had ties in the drug world too, of course, and one of his allies wasn't too fond of being turned down by Dedrick and his protection and services he could offer.

Pops only wanted his job but, as a show of good faith to one of his accomplices, he agreed to have Dedrick killed during the process.

Why not just kill him in the beginning and call it a day?

Pops had a twisted way of doing things.

He liked to cause the problem then swoop in and take care of it, one way or the other.

The same man Pops wanted in Dedrick's position was the man Dedrick had been chosen over in the beginning. Making Dedrick look bad with the affair was just a part of the show.

In the end, that's all this was.

I spotted Dedrick's car and stopped a few feet away from an abandoned building. Glancing around, it was dark, and it was obvious he'd left his car there.

Where the fuck did he go?

~***~

"Kemp?"

I stood there and so did she.

"Kemp?" she asked again.

Lava.

I wasn't sure how I'd ended up here—again.

But here I was. Looking at her as she stood in front of me.

I wasn't sure why I was here. I just woke up that morning and found myself on the highway to Virginia again since Satin would be busy with Dedrick for the day.

Lava walked closer to me.

I'd followed her from her house to the grocery store.

I'd parked right beside her and got out of the car before she did.

"I thought I was never going to see you again," she said, walking closer to me. Without thinking twice about it, she leaped into my arms.

I held her. Off the ground, close to my chest.

She talked and talked, but I didn't hear a word she'd said. I just wanted to hold her. I just wanted to feel her heart beating next to mine.

Even in that moment, I couldn't be sure what it was I felt for her.

It took me a minute but, finally, I put her down.

"What are you doing here? Is it safe for you to be here? I saw something about you on the news a while back. They arrested the bomber... Well, the man that took the blame. But it was you, right? You paid him or something, didn't you? You made him say it was him?"

She asked so many questions but all I could do was smile at her.

"I don't know what to say." she said.

"Shit. You said it all," I chuckled.

"Sorry…it's just…um…you know."

"Yeah, I know."

We looked into each other's eyes.

"Um, how old is—"

"I lost it. I was almost four months. No real reason why. Maybe my body is just tired of having kids."

I nodded at her. "Damn. Sorry to hear that."

"So, you and Satin…"

"Yeah. You and West?"

"Yeah. He opened an auto shop, a garage, or whatever you want to call it. He's actually still finishing up his schooling, but he has two other guys who works for him. I've been staying home. I'm enjoying it. I don't think I'll be going back to work anytime soon, if ever again. Well, West has been begging me to come and handle the paperwork. Are you still…you know…"

"Yes."

I knew she was asking if I was still involved in the unthinkable.

Lava touched the side of my face.

"I thought about you for a long time. After everything was all said and done, I wondered where you were and if you were okay."

"I'm okay," I assured her.

"Good."

I wanted to kiss her.

I wanted to, but I knew that I couldn't.

We both just stood there for a long while before she started to fiddle with her keys.

"I should probably go," Lava said. Then she opened her mouth to speak again. "I never got to say thank you. I don't know if you…um…if you killed Tokyo or not, and I don't want to know, but she's never been an issue again after I asked you… Well, you know. I just wanted to say thank you."

"You're welcome. I didn't kill her. She's alive. Somewhere. Probably still causing hell."

Lava looked relieved. "Good. After all she did, I still felt guilty…"

"No need. She's good. She just won't be a problem again." With her mentioning Tokyo, I wondered if she'd had any contact with her sister. Obviously, she still didn't know Tokyo had ran off to be with her. She damn sure wouldn't have been feeling any type of guilt if she knew the truth.

"How is your family? Thea? Your sisters?"

Lava smiled. "Thea had a baby! I still can't believe it. Her and Ying are finally thinking about coming home. She told me more about how you cleared up all his mess. I guess you just have your hands in everything, huh? Anyway, I'm hoping to see her soon. And my sisters are fine. One of my sisters lost her husband a while ago. Then she kind of fell off the map for a while. No one knew where she was or heard from her for months. She just popped back up. Now she's about to get married to one of her long-time co-workers. We've all told her she's moving way too fast, but Drea won't listen. I'm her matron of honor in the wedding. Everyone else is fine."

"Drea?"

"Yes. The oldest one."

I knew exactly who she was talking about.

I'd told her to stay away from Lava. After killing her husband, she and Tokyo were supposed to disappear. I'd made that clear. So, I was surprised to hear that she was back, and she was getting married to some other dude.

I thought about making good on my word and dealing with her as promised, but apparently, she was attempting to move on from her hidden issues with Lava.

It was obvious Lava still had no idea her sister was the brains behind Tokyo's actions, but Lava was in her wedding so apparently Drea had forgiven her and let it all go.

I'll let it ride for now.

If Lava ended up hurt again, I was coming for her.

"And the baby? Did Satin decide to keep it? I remembered you saying you were giving the baby to George, but—"

"No, Satin didn't keep the baby. And I decided not to give him to George. I decided to let him and his wife be. But he, the baby, is fine."

"Okay," she smiled.

"Okay."

It took her a long time to turn away from me, but finally, she did. She looked back at me over and over again, and I couldn't do or say anything.

All I could do was watch her.

All I could do was watch the woman I still adored slowly walk away from me.

~***~

LAVA

I forced myself not to look back at him again.

I wanted to, I really did, but I didn't.

Seeing Kemp had woken up something inside me I didn't know was still there. He had stirred up old feelings I thought were dead.

It had been almost a year since I'd seen him and months since he'd crossed my mind.

At first, I'd felt deceived by him, fooled, and even a little afraid of him and who he really was. After seeing him that day at the courthouse and after he'd help get my life back on track, all I felt for him was appreciation.

I knew he'd taken care of Detective Williams, and by taken care of him, I meant he was probably the reason he was dead, but I didn't care.

Surprisingly, I was thankful. Especially since life was back to normal and no other cops had come knocking at my door.

Wherever Tokyo was, since Kemp assured me she was still alive, I was thankful for whatever he'd done to make her stay away from me and my family.

It wasn't until I walked through the grocery store doors that I finally looked behind me again. A part of me had hoped he'd followed me inside, but he hadn't... *With his sexy self!*

He'd worn his dark, curly hair in that high ponytail on purpose. *He knows how I feel about that damn ponytail!* And the way he left the top three buttons of his shirt undone. I shivered remembering the sight of him.

I should've licked him.

I glanced down at my vibrating phone in my hand.

West.

West and I were better these days.

I couldn't say our marriage was the same because after what we'd gone through we had become different people, but our marriage was in a good place.

I'd lost the baby.

There was nothing that I'd done wrong, it was just something that happened. I wasn't worried. I wasn't stressed. At the time of the miscarriage, I was in a decent place, so I didn't blame West for my misfortune. Yet, he was right there. Helping me through it, being the loving husband he used to be. Not to mention he seemed much happier these days.

West had used some of our savings to open an auto shop. Since then, and to my surprised, he appeared to be more content doing oil changes and fixing brakes than he'd ever been putting out fires. He was a lot less stressed these days, and I liked seeing him smile.

"Don't forget the garlic bread," West said.

"I won't. And you said lasagna or spaghetti?"

"Either. Whichever one you have a taste for. I'll cook."

West now cooked for our family once a week and then he and I cooked together on Sundays.

The marital counseling that we had gone to for about six months, had really been worth the ridiculous amount of money. It had worked for us and it still was.

"Okay. I'll see you later when you get home."

"Love you, big head," West said.

"You better."

I hung up the phone and hurriedly paced around the grocery store.

Most of my loved ones wondered how I'd been able to forgive him.

It hadn't been easy.

For months, we had more bad days than good ones once everything had taken place and Tokyo was out of the picture. Some days we would argue until nightfall and other days he would hold me for hours while I cried.

Once we started going to counseling, I realized more than ever I should've left him. I shouldn't have fought so hard for someone who, at the time, didn't want to be kept. I should've let him go.

I'll never be that stupid again.

But now that things were better, I was happy I'd stayed. We were happy together, and with help, we'd saved our marriage.

Finally, I reached the checkout line. Just as I started to empty my cart, my phone vibrated again. Seeing it was Thea, I answered it in a hurry.

"Hello?"

"Bitch, it's hot, and I'm at your house. Where you at?"

My heart skipped a beat.

"My house? In Virginia? Wait…so you're back? Like…*back* back? In the U.S.? And you're at my house?"

I was so excited I could hardly breathe.

At this point, I hadn't physically seen Thea in almost a year in a half.

"Yes, bitch. We're back! You better hurry up before—"

"No! I'm on my way."

I hung up on her, and after paying for my groceries, I rushed out of the grocery store. Instinctively, I looked towards my car, hoping to see Kemp still standing beside it.

He wasn't.

Maybe I would never see him again.

Shaking away my thoughts, I loaded the car while smiling, eager to get to Thea.

Ying and Thea had stayed away, even after Kemp told me Ying was in the clear.

I remembered seeing it on the news.

I remembered cursing Thea out for not telling me the whole story, but she told me her husband told her not to. Apparently, he had been in a lot more trouble than he was telling her. Once his name was cleared, she confirmed Kemp was *the man*, and she was his number one fan for what he'd done for her husband.

She told me Ying had been referred to Kemp for help. Her husband didn't give her all the details, but she said she was sure Kemp had some dealings with some very powerful people. Possibly a few people in the government, but she couldn't be sure. All she knew was it had costed them millions to make Ying's money laundering problems go away. But she said it had been worth it.

Thea also finally told me Ying had stolen over fifty million dollars, and the man who had helped him steal the money was also the one who tried to take him down.

Nevertheless, with Kemp's help, Ying got away with his crimes just like Kemp had gotten away with his.

He'd told me out his own mouth he'd bombed the courthouse but someone else had taken the blame.

Why?

Probably money.

Who knows. I wasn't sure that I even wanted to.

All I knew was Thea was home!

Nothing else had come up about what she'd done to her stepfather again either, so she didn't have anything to worry about now that she was back.

My mind moved from Thea back to Kemp.

All the way home thoughts of him popped in and out my head.

He was still with Satin.

I guess that was a good thing.

I was surprised to hear she hadn't kept the baby.

I'd always wondered where the baby was.

George never spoke about the baby. At least, not around me, but he knew Satin was alive which meant he knew he had a child out there somewhere. I couldn't help but wonder how he felt about it. He'd always wanted kids, from my understanding, so I could only imagine he wanted to know where the baby was. Especially now that he was getting a divorce.

Recently, George's wife, Cheyenne, had left him.

She caught him cheating on her and said she had the feeling he had been for a very long time.

She was right.

At first, it was with Satin but once Satin was gone West revealed to me that he'd started cheating with someone else.

And because of it, he'd lost his wife.

In the back of my mind, I always wondered if West would have another affair. I couldn't say I trusted him completely or in the way I used to but, for the most part, I thought he'd learned his lesson.

I knew better than to say he would never do it again, but I also knew he was in this with me, and we were fighting for forever…together.

Even though Kemp was back in town.

I arrived at home to see a brand new, midnight blue Lexus in the driveway.

Thea.

I barely put the car into park before jumping out.

I saw the driver's side door open and out came Thea, running in my direction.

We jumped into each other's arms as though we were true first loves. I guess in a way we were.

"I missed you!" Thea said as I hugged her, almost wanting to cry. My cousin, my best-friend, was finally home!

"You must've been eating good as hell on that damn boat," I said to her once I was finally able to let her go. Thea had always been skinny, but she'd picked up some weight and it looked good on her.

"Where is she? Where is she?"

Thea laughed as I ran to the other side of the car and opened the door.

Baby Fiona cooed at the sight of me.

"Oh, my God! She's so cute and so juicy!" I squealed as I unbuckled her and picked her up. "Hey, baby, it's Auntie Lava," I called myself. "Aw, Thea, she's so precious. Is she walking yet?"

"Damn, bitch, who do you think I had a baby with? The *Energizer Bunny*? She's only seven months."

I couldn't help but laugh.

"Dang. Really? It just seems so long ago that you left."

"I was only about three months when you and Tokyo were going at it. I had her months later and now she's seven months. It's been almost a year since everything somewhat went back to the way that they used to be."

"Yeah. I know. Speaking of..." I handed Thea her baby. "You'll never believe who I just saw at the grocery store."

"Who?"

"Kemp."

"Kemp?"

I nodded then told her to head into the house while I grabbed the groceries.

It took a few minutes, but I got everything situated before we sat down on the couch in the living room while the baby crawled around on the floor.

"What the hell is Kemp doing back in town?"

I shrugged. "I don't know, but—"

"Uh uh. Don't even think about it!" Thea said. "Everything is back on track. Tokyo is only God knows where. You and West are doing fine. I'm sure Kemp is still with Satin. Shit, I don't know. If I had a little fling that looked like Kemp..." Thea laughed, taking a sip of the Kool-Aid I'd given her. Immediately, she frowned. "Girl, what the fuck is this? Here, go do something with this glass of diabetes! Damn, did you use a whole bag of sugar?"

"Thea!"

"Girl, that shit is nasty. Santa gotta' bring you a measuring cup for Christmas or something 'cause you too damn old not to know how to make Kool-Aid!" Thea snickered as a reaction to my laughing then she shook her head. "But like I was saying, don't start nothing. It won't be nothing."

"I'm not doing anything. I'm just saying... He looked so good, Thea."

"What else is new? He's always been sexy. Girl, when I saw him in Puerto Rico, glistening in that golden sun...I almost put one of my titties in his mouth," Thea giggled.

"Thea!"

"What? Shit? You know he fine! And I know he's off limits. But for real, you got what you wanted. You got West. That's what you wanted. Now, I don't know why in the hell you still wanted him, but you fought for him and you got him. So be happy and stay on the straight and narrow. Feel free to play with that *pussycat* whenever Kemp crosses your mind, but that's it. Just let it be," Thea preached, as I nodded.

I hated it when she was right.

~***~

SATIN

"I really enjoy talking to you," Dedrick said.

"I enjoy talking to you too," I answered honestly.

After our "chance" encounter at the restaurant and letting him take me out to dinner last week, we'd been talking all day, every single day. I had to admit the conversations we were having were quite refreshing.

He asked me things I'd never even thought about before. He asked me about my dreams and my purpose in life. He asked me about my thoughts and my deepest desires. Somehow, he saw past my beauty and desperately tried to see inside my heart, though I couldn't fully let him.

It was as though he was really trying to get to know me; the real me. And not just the lady I was pretending to be.

I was pretty sure I'd talked about more things with Dedrick here lately than I'd talked about with Kemp in a very long time. And lately, it seemed as though I was barely talking to him at all.

Kemp seemed to be on edge these last few days.

He always seemed to be up to something.

I knew my father had him tying up a few other loose ends, but it seemed to be something else that had him running around like a chicken with its head cut off. He wasn't saying much and he was always on the move, making it easy for Dedrick to have a lot of my time and attention.

"Hey?" I looked at Dedrick. "You spaced out on me for a second there. Is there something on your mind?"

I shook my head no.

Dedrick and I were seated in the middle of a crowded restaurant. Despite who he was, he was out in the open, saying we were just friends having a casual dinner. And with his wife, Carla, believing I was a journalist, I was sure if anyone approached her with suspicions she would correct them and say I was interviewing him to find out his thoughts on her success since I'd told her I would be.

But really, being seen with him, in public, was exactly what I needed. Us being seen together, often, would make the stories of our affair more believable.

"I don't want to offend you, but I have to ask you. Are those your real eyes?"

I nodded at him. "Yes. Do you want to see it on my license?"

He laughed. "No, that's not necessary. They're just so beautiful."

Of course, Kemp had a driver's license made with my current look and my current name, Sandra; the one that I was going by with Dedrick. And in the eye section, my eye color said hazel.

"You never talk about your husband..."

"There's not much to say. He was an asshole and then he died. The end."

"Wow. Doesn't seem like you miss him."

"I don't. Do you miss your wife?"

He looked at me with a confused expression, so I elaborated.

"Here. With me. Right now. Do you miss her?" I said to him softly, licking my red lips.

Dedrick took a sip of his drink, never taking his eyes off mine.

"If I'm being honest, no. She hasn't even crossed my mind."

Once I smiled at him and he grinned back, I knew I had him right where I wanted him. He had no idea what he was walking into. He had no idea he was making the biggest mistake of his life. But for the first time ever, something just didn't feel right.

****

Chapter Three

KEMP

I was waiting on Satin to text me.

Dedrick was at her apartment for the first time.

I was across the parking lot, staring out the window.
Mad, jealous, and a whole lot of other shit.

This was the hardest part.

No matter how many times we'd been down this road,
I still didn't like it. Knowing she was with another man still
made my blood boil.

Nine.

That's how many other man have touched my wife.

Nine.

I'd only had to kill two of them so far. Dedrick would
be the third. If it'd been up to me, I would've killed them
all. But nothing had ever been up to me.

Shit, maybe I wouldn't have killed any of them if the
choice had been mine.

Pops, Satin's father, almost never left Cairo. He trusted
me more than anyone else who worked for him, so I made
most of his moves.

The important ones anyway.

If someone needed to be paid off or kept quiet, that was my job. If someone needed to be "taken care of", again, he depended on me. You see, only Satin and I really knew what he was capable of, no matter how many people he had on his team.

Pops had doctors, lawyers, politicians, judges, cartel members, military personnel, entertainers, reporters, athletics, newspapers, pastors, stockbrokers, and everyone else in between in his back pocket. Anyone that could possibly be of any worth.

He'd spent years forming this huge network, following in his father's footsteps, who had been just as powerful before he died. This power trip, and Satin's family money, stretched back at least three generations that I knew of.

Pops was probably the worst of them.

He preached peace but that was a load of bullshit.

Everything was about him. It always has been.

Still, he never really got his hands dirty.

He just paid me or someone else to do it for him.

Satin's father always paid me for my services. He always paid Satin too. As though we were his employees and not his daughter and son-in-law. As though he believed money would make us forget about the things he asked us to do.

But I would never forget them.

I always wondered what made Pops approach my father about me marrying his daughter. He could've chosen anybody. Someone wealthy and a part of her world, but he picked me. As poor as we were, he picked me. I was sure it was all about control.

And for years, I did what I was told out of obligation. But I'd long since repaid my debt.

And me and my wife were on our way out.

My folks crossed my mind.

They were old, but I made sure they were comfortable. I hadn't seen them in a while, but they didn't have a care in the world. I'd always taken good care of them and my sister.

Before she died.

Rehema was my younger sister. My only sibling.

She'd begged to come to America to study.

And with Pop's help, we made it happen.

Rehema came to the U.S. and enrolled in college.

Satin and I watched out for her as much as we could. There were times where we had to be away from her for months at a time, but we always checked in.

Her last year of college we were in South Carolina, and she and Satin decided to have a girls' night out.

I stayed home. Well, what we were calling home at the time and watched basketball. I'd grown to love it over the years, though I'd never played. Never even dribbled a basketball.

Around two in the morning, I got the call.

Satin was screaming and crying, and I begged her to tell me what was wrong. She'd been driving them home, drunk, and swerved to miss a deer. She ran into a light pole and, Rehema, who hadn't been wearing her seatbelt, went through the windshield.

My sister Rehema died that night.

And we covered it up.

After getting there and seeing Satin passed out on one side of the car while Rehema laid dead on the ground on the other side, for the first time in a long time, I found it hard to function. It was a situation I couldn't control, but I didn't have time to grieve.

A few neighbors had heard the crash and came into the street. Before they could get too close and ask too many questions, our contacts at the police department pulled up and ushered them back into their homes. Moments later the medical help we had in town arrived. After loading Rehema and Satin inside of the ambulance, I followed them to a hidden location.

That's when it hit me.

Grief hit me hard as I held my sister in my arms.

I was used to feeling guilt for some of the things I did, but I hadn't really experienced heartache until that very moment. Still, I couldn't cry because Satin opened her eyes and immediately started to wail. In one of my weakest moments, I had to be strong for her.

I told her it wasn't her fault.

But wasn't it?

She knew to call me or a cab. She knew not to get behind the wheel of a car drunk but, in that moment, all I could do was comfort her.

Then we did what we had to do next.

We cleaned the mess.

No one but the people involved that night knew what actually happened to Rehema. We told our families Rehema had been the one driving and hit the pole. We left out the drinking and simply said she swerved to avoid the deer. We found out that she was pregnant, but we didn't know who the father was or if she even knew about the pregnancy. Her death was never reported, and her body was shipped back to my parents in Cairo for a proper burial.

We handled getting her withdrawn from college and made sure she was never reported as missing.

And just like that, my sister was gone.

And it was all because of my wife.

I'd told Lava a completely different story about that night at first. Then I told her a little of the truth in the end. I'd never told a soul what had really happened though, and I never would.

For a while after it all, Satin was touch and go.

She was depressed for weeks.

She'd sworn she would never drink again and for a while she didn't. Then she got drunk and made another fucked up choice. She'd gotten pregnant by George.

The sudden beep caused me to look down at my phone.

I read Satin's message. She said she couldn't do it. She couldn't have sex with Dedrick. She said she didn't want to. In the past, she wouldn't have hesitated to do what she needed to do for her father. That's how I knew she was fed up too.

Satin was a daddy's girl and her father, as horrible as he was, was her idol. He was the only person in the world she loved more than she loved me.

He loved the hell out of her too, which was why we were going to be able to get out of this.

She just had to push through. She just had to get the job done.

Come on, baby. We're almost done…

~***~

SATIN

I placed my phone down on the table after telling Kemp I would be headed across the parking lot in a few minutes.

Dedrick was still here.

I'd finally invited him to my apartment to take this whole thing between us to the next level.

We'd been talking, laughing, going to dinner, watching sunsets in his car, and even kissing for a few weeks now, but I couldn't bring myself to sleep with him.

It wasn't because I couldn't.

It was because… I really *wanted* to.

I actually wanted to give Dedrick the *business*, and it freaked me out!

I liked him. I really liked him. And I knew I wasn't supposed to.

I liked spending time with him. I liked the way he made me feel. Most of all, I liked the way he looked at me. When Dedrick looked at me, he saw something in me I didn't even see when I looked at myself. He was constantly giving me compliments and showering me with words of hope and undeserving gratitude. He made me feel so good.

I had a camera waiting to record us in my room. I'd already told him I liked to get freaky and that I wanted to videotape the act. At first, he was hesitant but, the more I teased him, he was all in. He had no idea I just wanted an opportunity to get him on camera with me, so I could later use it to destroy him later.

I just couldn't do it.

I didn't want to hurt him, and I damn sure didn't want Kemp to kill him.

Dedrick was funny. He was smart and so sweet. I mean, sure he was a married man and planning to cheat on his wife with me, but outside of that, he was the perfect guy.

If there was such a thing.

I wanted Dedrick so bad I could taste him, and usually, oral sex was only reserved for my husband. But I had this dying urge to please him in every way. I was just so scared of what would follow.

"I really have to get up in the morning," I lied, trying to fight my desires.

"Okay."

Dedrick stood up, and I stared at him with eyes full of lust.

"So, tell me something." Dedrick tapped the tip of my nose with his index finger. "When I'm not around, do I ever cross your mind?"

He came closer to me once I was on my feet, and the muscles in my vagina tightened.

We both breathed hard. I playfully pushed away from him, but he pulled me back into his arms and close to his chest.

"Answer my question," he chuckled.

"Um. Um. What was it again?"

I looked up at him, towering over me as he waited for him to ask me the question again, but he didn't. Instead, he kissed me.

Just as our tongues started to intertwine, my phone vibrated against the coffee table. It was probably Kemp wondering what was taking me so long.

I attempted to pull away from Dedrick, but he wouldn't let up. And for some strange reason, I didn't want him to.

We kissed for what seemed like eternity then he started to push me towards the couch.

"You have to believe me, I've never cheated on my wife," he said between kisses.

I stopped kissing him.

Obviously.

Otherwise he would've known he'd said the wrong thing at the wrong time.

All he'd done was remind me this wasn't real. That he wasn't mine.

"Then why are you here? With me?"

Dedrick shook his head. "For some crazy reason, there's nowhere else I would rather be."

Those were the last words he said before he laid me down on the sofa and I allowed him to have his way with me.

Dedrick took his time with me. He touched me all over. Kissed me in places that had never been kissed.

Sex with him wasn't quite like sex with Kemp, but it was fulfilling. I'd enjoyed it. And though with other men I usually felt unclean, with him I didn't.

Once we were finished, and after a few words, I lied to him again about having to get up early, so he got himself together and kissed me goodbye. When he left, I placed my back up against the door and took a deep breath just as my phone chimed.

Rushing towards the table, I picked it up.

Kemp had called and texted a few times. He'd asked where I was and if I was okay. I could see from the messages if I didn't get over there soon he would think something had gone wrong.

I sent him a quick text then I hurried to the bathroom to take a quick shower. In less than twenty minutes, I was bathed, in pajamas, and heading out my apartment.

As I got closer to Kemp's building, I could see him standing in the door of his apartment, waiting for me. I knew he was going to want details, and I planned to tell him everything…except for the last part.

I knew what had to be done.

I knew there was no way around it.

I just needed time to think.

I needed time to figure out a way to save Dedrick.

Him losing his job and ruining his life and marriage was one thing. I could live with that.

But I just couldn't let him die.

As I got closer, Kemp entered his apartment and a few seconds later I entered behind him, knowing I was about to do something I'd never done before.

For the first time ever, I was going to lie to him.

~***~

LAVA

"What's on your mind, baby?" West asked.

Kemp.

Of course, I couldn't say that.

I hadn't been able to stop thinking about him.

It seemed as though I was looking for him everywhere I went. Waiting for him to pop up again or hoping he would approach me from behind.

But I hadn't seen him.

Not since that day at the grocery store.

"Nothing, baby. Just tired."

West offered to get the kids ready for bed, so I headed to our bathroom to run myself a bath.

After all that had happened, I still remembered the way Kemp kissed me. The way he touched me. The way I felt when he was inside me.

It had been a while since West and I had been intimate. Between him coming home late from the shop or school and me being exhausted from a long day with the kids or one of the kids somehow ending up in our bed, it had been a month since we'd had sex. And at least two weeks since I'd even seen him naked—maybe even three.

But tonight was the night.

He was going to give me some, whether he was in the mood or not. Hopefully, hot, nasty sex with West would take my memories of sex with Kemp far, far away.

Or maybe it would only remind me of who he wasn't.

Grabbing a razor, I turned on some music, turned off the water and got into the bathtub with thoughts of sex and Kemp still floating around in my head. Instantly feeling relaxed, I rested my head against the edge of the bathtub and closed my eyes.

I felt guilty for wanting to entertain my thoughts of Kemp, but my mind didn't give me much of a choice.

I knew he was bad.

I knew he killed people and only God knows what else he was involved in.

But who was I to judge?

I'd done some horrible things to get back at Tokyo, helped burn down the mayor's house, and not to mention, I almost killed Satin.

Hell, I wasn't exactly an angel myself.

My last sexual encounter with Kemp crossed my mind.

I remembered looking into his eyes as I touched myself. I remembered watching him, watching me as he stroked every inch of his *wood*.

With my eyes still closed, without my permission, my left hand started to caress my nipple on my left breast and my right hand found its way through the water to my thumping clitoris.

I could see him. I could smell him as my fingers started to move in a circular motion. Visions of his body, his lips, and even his sexy ass man-bun had my hormones racing all over the place. My fingers were desperately trying to keep up.

My body temperature started to rise, and I found it harder and harder to suppress my moans.

"Oooh…yes…yes…" I moaned loudly. "Yes…oooh…Kemp…"

"What the fuck you just say?"

My eyes popped open so fast you would've thought that I'd heard a gunshot.

West was standing there in the bathroom, completely naked as though he had been watching me please myself for a while.

I sat up in a hurry, splashing water all over the floor.

"I asked you a question. What did you just say?" West growled. His before hard dick slowly softened as he stared at me.

He huffed. "So, you were touching yourself while thinking about another man, right? In my house?"

I shook my head no.

"You still fucking him Lava?"

"What? No! No. I…"

I didn't know what to say. I stood up to get out of the tub, but West held up his hand.

"No. You stay. I'll go," he said as he slammed the bathroom door behind him.

Ah hell. Here we go…

~***~

"He'll get over it," Thea said.

I'd been riding around with her all day, viewing houses since she and Ying were looking for a new one to buy. They still had their old house, but they had tenants. Instead of renting something until they moved out, Thea said she'd just rather purchase a new one.

Ying hadn't come back to the States yet. He was still somewhere on the cruise ship he'd purchased. Thea said he wouldn't be joining them for another month or so once he was done meeting with a few potential buyers of the ship. She was hoping he sold it as soon as possible, and she was hoping to have a new home ready for him when he returned.

For now, she was staying with her mother—my aunt—though I'd been begging her to stay with me.

"He hasn't said a word to me in three days. Not one single word. We were doing so good. I can't tell you the last time we had an argument before this one."

Thea shrugged.

"Hell, it's not like you were actually having sex with the man." Thea thought about it. "Hell no, scratch that. I would fuck Ying all the way up if I caught him whacking off and moaning another woman's name! West should've punched you in the top of your damn head!" She laughed. I didn't. "But give it time. He will get over it. Hell, he had been sleeping with Tokyo for how long? I'm sure he has his moments where he thinks about her too."

Tokyo.

I hadn't seen her. No one had heard from her. And I damn sure didn't spend my days thinking about her.

I'll admit, after it all went down in the beginning, I'd tried to look for her on social media a few times, but I couldn't find her. That was another reason I'd thought maybe Kemp had…

Thea stopped driving. I looked at the house we were parked in front of.

It was George and Cheyenne's house.

"They're selling their house?"

Thea shrugged. "It's on my realtor's list."

I figured Cheyenne was probably selling it because of the divorce.

Wait…is that…

George and Cheyenne came out of the house—together.

"Hey girl," Cheyenne chimed at me. George spoke too.

He briefly asked about West then he and Thea headed inside.

I looked at Cheyenne.

"I thought the two of you were…"

"Ugh, girl. We were. We have so much to catch up on, but I've just been so busy with trying to fix things with George." She looked at me as though she was trying to see if I approved. "West talked us into going to see a counselor. The same one the two of you used. She's good."

"That she is," I agreed.

"We are going to give it one more try. He stopped seeing her, his mistress, and he admitted to having another affair with another woman before her."

I held my breath to see if she would mention the baby, but she didn't.

"He put everything out there in the open. He was honest. I guess trying it one more time may not be so bad?" she asked for reassurance.

"Hey, it's your marriage. If West and I can bounce back and get on track, anybody can," I said.

Cheyenne hesitated. "I just can't help but to feel like my infertility is part of the problem. If I'd been able to get pregnant, he would've never cheated on me. I just know he wouldn't have. And I tried. I did. It's not my fault. He's always wanted kids so bad, and I just know we would've been happy if I could've just given him a child," she said.

"Still, he's a grown ass man. He made his own choices. He decided to cheat because he wanted to. It has nothing to do with you."

She nodded. "Well, we can adopt. That's what we've agreed to do. So, we're selling the house, starting fresh in a new home, and we're going to adopt a baby," she said.

I beamed at her then I gave her a big hug. Once she embraced me, I could feel how tensed, nervous, and unsure she was, so I gave her a little more encouragement.

"Everything is going to be fine. You'll see," I said to her.

We stood outside and talked for a while until Thea and George came back out the house.

We all said a few more words to one another then Thea and I got into her car and drove away.

Thea waited until we'd turned off their street and she spoke.

"That George is a goddamn man-whore, I tell you!"

I whipped my neck around to face her so fast I almost gave my whiplash.

"Girl, no, he didn't…."

"Girl, yes, he did! And he a bold little something too! Came right out and asked me for some pussy. Offered to pay for it and everything…in *their* house. With his wife right outside."

"You're lying, Thea!"

"Chile, you know I'm not. I wouldn't fuck him with my worst enemy's pussy! With his ugly self. She better leave his ass! And she had better do it soon!"

Thea turned up the radio.

I frowned.

I felt bad for Cheyenne.

She was so hopeful, only to soon be let down again.

I contemplated whether or not it was my place to tell her, and it caused me to think about my own life, marriage, and a few other things.

I mean, at the end of the day, does anyone ever really change?

~***~

KEMP

"He wants me to go away with him for the weekend. Tonight," Satin said to me.

"Where? I'll make sure I'm there."

She hesitated. "Virginia."

I looked at her.

"He has some kind of conference there, and he wants me to go with him. Of course, there will be a lot of press, so I'll just be at his hotel. I'm in full-blown mistress position now," Satin confirmed.

Virginia.

Lava.

I hadn't been back there since seeing her that day. Seeing her hadn't been good for me. Seeing her confused me. And I told myself I was going to stay away.

"Babe?"

I looked at Satin.

She looked so beautiful. She had the contacts out her eyes, causing me to realize how much I missed her natural beauty.

"I'll be right behind you, baby," I said to her.

"Um huh, I bet you will. I swear you better not make your way to Lava or—" she threatened.

"Baby, I won't."

We were still trying to get back on good terms, so I knew if I did make my way to see Lava I wouldn't be able to tell Satin about it.

"I know you can't seem to shake her but don't make me hurt you…or her."

Satin's face was tensed, but somehow, she was still cute as fuck. Even when she was mad.

"Baby, now you know," I teased.

"I know what, huh?"

She grinned once I picked her up and held her in my arms. She wrapped her legs around my waist.

"Since we're keeping it real, sure Lava has crossed my mind a time or two. Why? Your guess is as good as mine. But she ain't you. You ain't ever got to worry about me leaving you. You know that. And with everything going as planned, we won't have to worry about much of anything anymore. No more purpose. No more jumping at your father's command. Just me and you. Me fucking you, and sucking you, and loving you…" I kissed her.

"Forever," she finished my sentence.

"Forever."

We shared a few more kisses, but she refused to give me some pussy, saying she had to get her stuff together to meet Dedrick soon.

Once she was out of the door, I made a few calls to finish getting a few things in order. Satin and I had a few millions in the bank, offshore accounts, and a stash at my folks' house inside of the basement walls.

I wanted to surprise her with a beach house when all this was said and done.

We'd been talking about the Cayman Islands for some time now, and there wasn't a doubt in my mind there was where we would end up.

I could see her now, walking on the beach with the wind blowing through her hair…once it grew back.

She was my forever.

She was my heart.

She was mine.

Even if Lava had a piece of my mind.

~***~

A few hours later I was arriving in Virginia.

Satin had long since reached the state with Dedrick, and I headed to the same hotel they were staying in to check-in.

The city where the conference was being held was about a twenty-minute drive from where Lava lived.

I could get there in fifteen.

Satin would be tied up with Dedrick all weekend, so I was on her time with calls and texts. I had plenty of time to spare.

And I knew exactly where I was going to be.

Once I checked-in, I texted only the room number to Satin's phone, so she knew I was there.

She sent back a thumbs-up emoji. With that, I walked right back out the hotel and drove towards the highway.

Fifteen-minutes later I pulled up in front of Lava's house.

It was late summer, but the kids were already back in school I supposed.

Only her jeep was in the driveway.

After seeing her, I'd been tempted to call her, so I already had her new phone number. I took one of the other phones out of my glove compartment and dialed her number.

"Hello?"

"Look outside."

Seconds later Lava appeared on the front porch with the phone still to her ear.

"Hi," she said once she saw me.

I just stared at her and held the phone.

"I need to talk to you," she said.

"Follow me."

I hung up and she hurried back into the house then came out with her keys and her purse. I watched her get into her jeep and then I pulled off.

My phone started to vibrate in my hand.

Shit.

It was Satin.

"Hello?"

"He's gone. He said he will be back later, so I'm stuck here in the room, wishing I was with you," she said.

Damn.

That's what I like to hear.

I had to get Lava out of my system.

"Where you at?" Satin asked.

"Driving."

"Driving where?"

"I don't know yet," I answered honestly.

"Kemp…"

"Trust me," I said to her. She and I knew the only people we could truly ever trust and depend on was each other. I knew by saying the words she would back off, but I also knew I couldn't wait to stop driving so I could get close to Lava.

"Okay," Satin said. "I love you."

I told her what she needed to hear then I hung up. I decided to head to the bar. Satin and I didn't personally own it, but our organization did. Basically, Pops did. I pulled into the parking lot, headed around to the back of the bar, and used my spare key to open the back door.

Lava silently followed me, as we made our way to the back office. I sent a text to Hamid, the man that was the actual face and *acting* owner of the bar, as well as *my* employee, letting him know I was using the office and wasn't to be disturbed.

Finally, I turned to face her.

She stood there as though she was nervous. I could tell she was waiting for me to say something. When I didn't, she did.

"I haven't been able to stop thinking about you since I saw you," Lava confessed.

I didn't respond.

"It's funny. I've been happy. I was content. And then I saw you. Whatever I'm feeling for you, just doesn't make sense. I love my husband. I fought for him. Almost killed for him. Yet, I find myself sitting around, thinking about you. Thinking about us. Thinking about—"

I touched the side of her face, and she closed her eyes.

Maybe it was a sexual attraction for us. She was the first woman I've ever touched since marriage other than Satin. I was the first man she'd given herself to since being with her husband.

Maybe this was a physical thing.

There was only one way to find out.

"Give it to me," I growled.

"What?"

I pulled her closer and palmed her ass.

"Give it to me. It's what we both want. Shit, maybe it's what we need. You go your way, I'll go mine. I won't come back to Virginia again."

Lava shook her head.

"I can't, Kemp. I can't."

I lowered my face closer to hers.

"After all the mess and all of the work to fix my marriage… I can't."

I kissed her.

She wasn't the only one that was married.

Satin would kill me—and Lava if she knew where I was and what we were about to do.

The first time around, she felt guilty for getting pregnant, so she let the shit ride.

This time, I doubt it.

Despite what Satin thought, Lava hadn't been some type of get back because I was angry at her for getting pregnant by that clown, George. I'd already run into Lava at the bar before Satin found out the baby news. Well, at least before she told me.

And when I saw Lava again with Thea, I gave her my number because I'd wanted to.

I wanted to talk to her.

I wanted to know her.

I didn't think we would take it to the bedroom, but once we did, I couldn't seem to get enough of her.

And right here, right now, I wanted her again.

Lava didn't stop me from kissing her, nor did she pull away from me.

We kissed for a long time.

It was funny because when I was with Satin I couldn't stop thinking about Lava. Now that I was with Lava, I couldn't stop thinking about Satin.

"No, we can't," Lava's mouth said, but her body said something different. I lifted her dress. She allowed it. And when I tugged on her panties, she allowed that too.

I pushed her towards the office desk and bent her over.

My *Johnson* was so hard it felt like it was going to break in half, but I managed to put on a rubber. Before she could stop me, I went in deep, all the way to her guts, causing her to call out my name.

"Kemp," Lava moaned, as I stroked her slowly.

She resisted for only a couple of seconds and then she got into the mood. As I stroked her, she threw her ass against my stomach over and over again.

I smacked it and then I grabbed a fistful of her hair and stopped playing around. I went to work.

The room was filled with my constantly ringing phone, Lava's moans, and the slapping noise our colliding bodies continued to make. She was so wet. I knew she wanted me. I had to space my feet a little further apart, so I could navigate through her wetness and taunt the bottom of her stomach.

Finally, with nothing on my mind but busting a good one, I stroked until Lava's body told me she was ready. After three more pumps, so was I.

I met her at the finish line.

Shit!

I missed that shit.

Once I stepped back from her, Lava stood up and pulled down her dress.

Breathing hard and in a panic, she searched for her panties.

I just watched her.

Waiting to see what she would say. But she didn't say anything. She didn't even look at me.

She just tucked her panties inside her bra and headed for the office door.

She waited there for me to get myself together, and still without talking or looking directly at me, she followed me towards the back door.

"Lava," I called out to her once we were outside, but still, she said nothing.

She'd barely shut her car door before she started it and drove away.

Damn.

~***~

SATIN

I was pissed!

I was in jail… For nothing!

I'd tried calling Kemp before I'd gotten locked up, but he hadn't been answering the phone.

Earlier, when I hung up with him, I already knew what he was up to.

He was going to see Lava.

I wasn't stupid.

My gut told me I was going to have to show up and turn all the way up on his ass, but I was trying to let him sort through his feelings on his own.

He just better not fuck her!

Anyway, after hanging up with Kemp, I decided to take a bath.

There I was, relaxing, enjoying the bubbles when I heard the hotel door open.

I called out to Dedrick, but Dedrick wasn't the one who appeared in front of the bathroom door.

It was Carla…his wife.

I'd hurried out the tub just as she started to go off. She'd said she'd gotten a key from the front desk and came up to surprise him but there I was to her surprise instead.

She recognized me, remembered me, and she was furious I was there, obviously fooling around with her husband.

She said she'd had the feeling he was creeping around lately, but to find out it was me was an insult.

I didn't even try to explain anything to her. All I could think about was if it was too early for everything to come out in the open, especially since I still didn't have a clue on how to keep Dedrick alive.

Carla fussed and fussed, and still, I said nothing.

I guess that pissed her off even more because once I walked passed her she attacked me from behind.

I didn't have a choice but to fight back.

Of course, I'd been trained to fight, but I tried not to hurt her. For the most part, wet and naked, I tried to restrain her, but I had to give her a two-piece here and there.

We went at it until Dedrick came into the room screaming and pulled us a part. He'd forgotten his wallet in his other jacket pocket, which was the only reason he'd come back so soon.

Immediately, his wife turned on him. While they went at it, I hurried to get dressed. Carla noticed I thought the heat was off of me, so she called 9-1-1 from her phone just as there was a knock on the room door.

None of us headed towards it. While Carla was talking to the police, Dedrick shouted a few things at me just as hotel staff and security opened the room door with their spare key.

Dedrick tried to stay calm and tried to calm down his wife, but she was in a rage.

I tried to get out of the room, but hotel management and security wouldn't move out my way since Carla was screaming I attacked her.

She started spitting some legal mumbo jumbo at them, causing them to hold me. Once the police arrived, she lied and told them I assaulted her too. I tried to tell them she attacked me and hit me first, but she was the one with the busted lip and the bloody nose so off to jail I went.

Before the police had even gotten there, I'd pressed on Kemp's number over and over again, but he hadn't answered. Even right before they put me in handcuffs, I called him again. Still, he hadn't picked up.

He hadn't answered my calls because he was with that bitch!

Once they booked me, instead of using my one phone call to call Kemp again, I called one of my father's phones; the one that was only for emergencies. He'd had that number for years, so of course I'd memorized it. And yes, I'd called him just to get Kemp in trouble.

I knew he was going to call Kemp, and I could only imagine that the conversation wouldn't be pretty.

Good.

Kemp and my father were extremely close.

Kemp was his son, his partner, his eyes and his ears. But I was his heart. When he found out Kemp was nowhere to be found while I was fighting and going to jail, he was livid!

I would've loved to be a fly on the wall just to hear what he was going to say to Kemp.

Now, I wasn't a fool.

Of course, I didn't tell my father I thought Kemp was with another woman, but I made it clear how upset I was that Kemp hadn't been there to come to my rescue.

I hung up with my father, knowing one way or another, help was on the way.

Whether he sent Kemp to get me out or called whoever his contact was at the police station to let me go.

But it was taking forever!

I kept thinking about everything and what would come next. I wondered if Carla was going to leave Dedrick. I wondered if she would expose the affair and do all of the hard and dirty work for us. I wondered if he would immediately resign. And strangely, I wondered how long I would have to save him.

This wasn't supposed to happen.

Surely, his wife would go public about his affair and tell the press. I was sure the folks at the hotel would do the same since they all knew exactly who Dedrick was.

I sat in the cell, disgusted, until finally, the officer called my name. Slowly, I walked towards him.

He opened the cell and led me to where Kemp was waiting for me.

I could see him, pacing back and forth with his hair thrown to one side. When he looked up and saw me, he rushed towards me.

"Go," the officer said.

He took off the handcuffs.

"That's it. I don't have to sign anything…"

He winked at me. "Go."

Kemp touched my arm, and I pulled away from him.

Hurriedly, we walked out the police station and Kemp grabbed my arm again. Again, I snatched it away from him.

"Baby, I'm so sorry. What happened? I'm sorry. I—"

"You were too busy with Lava! Weren't you?"

Kemp's face was stern, and it didn't change from my comments.

"You know what? Yeah, you are sorry! Today, you were a sorry ass excuse for a husband!"

I turned to walk away from him.

He didn't say anything, but I could hear him following behind me.

I guess maybe I was overacting.

I was out of jail, the affair was out, and everything was fine. Well, almost everything.

I got into Kemp's car and fastened my seatbelt.

"Satin."

"Were you with Lava?"

Kemp didn't reply.

"Were you with Lava!"

Kemp exhaled.

"Yes."

"I knew it!" I screamed. I opened his car door and got out. Kemp got out behind me and started trying to explain.

"Did you fuck her?" I turned around to face him. I was so upset I wanted to cry, but I didn't. I just wanted to hear his response.

"Did you fuck her, Kemp?" I growled.

He looked at me with remorse.

"Yes," he said.

Oh, really?

That bitch is dead!

~***~

LAVA

"No, you didn't!"

I shook my head at Thea.

She was chastising me and smiling at the same time.

I was so confused.

"How in the hell did that happen?"

"He called me out of the blue, told me to come outside, then asked me to follow him. I followed him to the bar. And...I don't know how it happened. I didn't mean to! I feel so bad, Thea!"

"Girl, but I bet it felt so damn good!" Thea stuck out her tongue.

"Thea! I'm serious!"

"Okay, okay, okay. Well, at least you feel bad about it. Maybe that means you won't do it again."

"I'm not doing it again! All the work we put in counseling this past year, and now, I feel like I failed. I have to tell West."

"*Shhhiiittt*...you don't have to tell West a motherfucking thing! Girl, just tell God and call it a day! You said you weren't going to see him or have sex with him again so let that be that. It was a mistake. They happen sometimes. Umph...I'd love to have a "Kemp" kind of mistake right now," Thea rolled her hips. "Hell, I miss my husband. My coochie is begging for some dick on a stick, if you know what I mean."

I shook my head. "Any news on when he's coming?"

"Soon. He sold the ship a few days ago. Since our renters needed to break their lease, due to an emergency with her parents on the west coast, we're going to go ahead and move back into our old house. Hopefully, he'll be home sometime next week," Thea confirmed. "But I meant what I said. Don't tell West. And, girl, next time you see Kemp's fine ass…run!" She snickered. "How he just gonna pop up slanging dick like that? I mean, damn! He came back like 'hey…how you doing…let me just stick the head in!' Where they do that at?"

I couldn't help but to laugh at her.

She was so stupid!

And so was I.

I tuned her out, as she continued to talk.

The thing was, I didn't know if I felt guilty because I'd had sex with Kemp or guilty because I'd liked it.

I'd damn near wanted to start running to get away from him. I hadn't known what to say or what to do. I felt so bad, yet so good, all at the same time.

That man is the damn Devil!

"Lava?" Thea snapped. "You was thinking about Kemp, wasn't you?" She grinned.

I rolled my eyes at her. Once West pulled in with the kids, she packed up to leave.

The kids greeted me then disappeared.

I followed West towards the bedroom.

"Hey."

"Hey," he said.

"How was your day?"

"It was fine," he said dryly.

I exhaled then I started to take off my clothes.

"Make love to me," I said once I was naked.

West looked at me confused.

"Make love to your wife," I said to him.

The kids were screaming and jumping in the next room, but still, I ignored them and walked closer to West.

"Make love to me," I said to him again, seductively.

West came close to me.

"No. Make love to yourself…and don't forget to invite Kemp again this time."

I frowned, knowing that my marriage was on the line. *Again.*

****

Chapter FOUR

KEMP

I fucked up.

Satin was giving me her ass to kiss, and no matter what I tried to do or say, she just wasn't trying to hear it.

Telling her I fucked Lava probably wasn't the best move, but in the moment, I had to be honest with her.

So, I told her.

She was insulted. She was furious. And she'd asked me the same questions over and over again.

Questions I didn't really have an answer to.

Why?

Why did I have sex with Lava?

I don't know.

I wanted to. I felt like I needed to. Like maybe getting with her just one more time would keep her off my mind.

That hadn't worked.

I still thought about her. Not every day though.

I was too busy trying to fix things with Satin, but nothing was working.

She kept screaming about how she only slept with other men because she *had* to, but I'd fucked Lava because I *wanted* to.

To her, it made all the difference in the world.

She wanted to know what it was about her.

Why I couldn't seem to forget about her?

What was it that Lava had that she didn't?

I couldn't answer those questions either.

"Are you hungry?"

Satin just sat on the other end of the phone.

For now, we were waiting, watching to see what Dedrick's wife was going to do. To see if she was going to take his affair public before figuring out what we needed to do next.

It had been a few days, and he hadn't reached out to Satin. Every night I'd been following him home. Satin had tons of text messages and pictures of them in her phone that we were planning to use once their affair went public. Initially, we were going to have our reporter friends snap a picture of them on down the line. Run a "who is this woman" article, with the photo of Satin and Dedrick being a little too close.

Then we were going to pretend as though her purse was stolen with her phone inside. Allowing the text messages and pictures to be exposed by "thief". At that point, we would leak it all and things would go downhill from there. That was the plan. But having his wife catch them and leak the story with what she saw was better.

It was easier.

So, for now, we were waiting.

If Dedrick never talked to Satin again, and if his wife stayed quiet, we would figure out what to do next. Either way, I was going to do what had to be done.

I was going to kill him.

Satin and I wouldn't be free until I did.

We told Pops what was going on. It was his idea for us to wait around and see what was next.

That day that Satin had gone to jail, he'd called me just as I'd gotten into the car from being with Lava, and he'd wanted answers. I simply told him I'd been at the bar checking on a few things and I'd left my cell in the car. He didn't ask to many question. He knew we had a few things tied into the bar, which was why we'd purchased it in the first place. He simply told me to stop what the fuck I was doing and get to the jailhouse to get his daughter.

"Are you hungry? I can go get something, and you can come over here," I said to her.

Satin still said nothing.

She just hung up.

I called her back twice. When she didn't answer her phone, I ordered pizzas. One to be delivered at my apartment and one to be taken to hers.

In the middle of texting another apology, a number popped up on the screen and I said them aloud.

"2-0-2-4-6-5…."

Lava.

"Hello?" she asked as soon as I picked it up.

"Lava."

"Kemp."

Silence.

"What we did the other day…that can never happen again."

"Okay," I responded.

"I'm so disappointed in myself. I don't know what I was thinking. I don't know what draws us to each other, and I don't know why I…just...please, if you care about me or whatever it is, please don't contact me or show up again."

"Okay."

She waited to see if there was anything else I needed to say. There wasn't.

"That's it? That's all you have to say? No reason why you showed up out of nowhere? No reason why you're back in Virginia? Or why you came to see me? Or why we—"

"No."

I didn't know what she wanted me to say.

I couldn't explain why I wanted her. I just did.

Lava exhaled loudly and then she said her favorite words. "Goodbye Kemp."

We hung up just as the doorknob started to turn.

Satin walked in.

I looked at her.

She didn't say anything to me. She walked to the back of the apartment, and just as I stood up, she appeared in the living room again. After rolling her eyes at me, still silent and holding her hair dryer, she walked right back out the front door, slamming it hard as hell.

I couldn't do a damn thing but laugh.

That's my baby.

And whether she wanted to be or not…

Lava was too.

~***~

SATIN

I knocked on the front door.

I waited a while and when no one answered I knocked again. This time I knocked hard like I was the police.

Finally, I heard her yell and the door flew open.

Lava.

At first, I couldn't read her.

I wasn't sure if she didn't recognize me or if she was just shocked to see me.

I smirked at her and folded my arms across my chest.

"Satin?"

"The one and only," I snarled.

She looked nervous.

I assumed her husband was home because she stepped out onto the front porch, closing the door behind her.

Kemp wasn't the only one that knew how to find people. I'd found out where she lived, and I'd decided to pay her a little visit.

I was here to put an end to my *other woman* issues.

Sure, I sounded stupid after I'd spent years sleeping with other people's husbands, but I didn't care.

I was done.

We were done.

And Kemp was mine!

"So, you fucked my husband—*again*."

She started to blink rapidly. She opened her mouth to speak, but I interrupted her.

"I'll hurt you. You do know that, don't you?"

She looked as though she didn't know what to say. I couldn't say she looked scared. But she should be.

"I mean, you did try to kill me once. So, the way that I see it…I still owe you one."

"I didn't try to kill you. It was an accident. I—"

I held up my hand in her face.

"Mine won't be! He's my everything. And I'll never let another woman take him from me. You of all people should know exactly what that means. This is the first and the last time I'm going to say this. Stay the hell away from *my* husband!"

The veins in Lava's neck started to bulge.

Is she getting upset?

"Just so you know, he came looking for me. I was fine. I was happy. I don't want him. I don't need him. So, this little conversation, is a conversation that you should be having with *your* husband. I'm just fine over here with my own. Thanks."

"Would your husband like to tell my husband 'thanks' for 'scratching that itch' you had the other day? Where is he? I'll be happy to relay the message."

Lava snarled.

I smirked.

Even with an attitude she was pretty, but so was I. There had to be something else he saw in her. Something beyond the surface that I just couldn't see.

"I'm not sure what he sees in you, but if he ever comes your way again, you'd better remember this little conversation. Because you don't want me to have to come back here again. Next time, I won't be coming to talk," I threatened then I turned to walk away from her.

She didn't say anything.

Not one single word.

I got into my car, and as I drove away, she was still standing on her front porch watching me.

I exhaled.

I was pretty sure I'd made myself clear.

And I would make good on my threats if I had too.

Though secretly, I was hoping my words had been enough.

Hopefully, she would just stay away from him until I could get him far away from her.

As I drove towards the highway, my phone started to ring over and over again.

It was Kemp.

I wasn't sure if Lava had called or texted him about my little visit, but I didn't care. I ignored his calls and called Dedrick instead.

I hadn't heard from him since the day I'd gone to jail.

I hadn't seen anything in the blogs or in the paper about our affair, so I was guessing his wife hadn't said anything to anyone. Neither had the hotel staff that was present that day.

The phone rang a few times, but Dedrick didn't answer.

I hated to say it, but I missed him.

I missed his conversation and how I felt on the inside whenever he was around.

Maybe my feelings were similar to what Kemp felt when he was with Lava. The only difference is, though I wanted to save his life and felt there was something there, he wasn't my husband. And never would I choose him over Kemp.

Kemp started to call my phone. *Again*. Instead of answering, I turned up the radio.

I was still mad at him, but I was going to forgive him. *Eventually*.

Kemp and I had done things together that we pretended not to remember. We'd done things to people only the two of us could relate to or understand. I'd ruined plenty of marriages. Kemp had plenty of blood on his hands. Even if he tried, he would never be able to forget the things he'd done.

We belonged together.

Despite all the bad, I couldn't see myself being with anyone but him.

But for now, I wanted to make him sweat.

Though I couldn't hear it over the music, I glanced down at my phone again just in time to see it was still ringing. But it wasn't Kemp who was calling this time.

It was my father.

I came from a long line of wealth.

My family owned properties and land all over Egypt, thanks to my great-great-grandfather's early business ventures.

And my father was…*is*…a very bad man.

In the beginning he'd tried to hide it, but once I agreed to work with him he hadn't had a choice but to reveal himself to me.

Money and power fueled him. I was convinced they were the two things that kept him living from day to day. Not me, not my mother, not our family. But his need to be as rich as he could be and in control.

I hadn't been forced to join his movement.

In the beginning, he actually told me no. But I'd wanted to. I'd wanted to make a difference. I'd wanted to help. I'd believed in his purpose and what he was trying to do for our people… Until I found out I had it all wrong.

Working for him wasn't anything like I'd thought it would be.

I remember the first time I had to do a "job".

He told me what he needed me to do. He told me he was sending me in to get close to the rich and powerful. To find out things he needed to know.

I thought it would be easy. It wasn't. All of the training in the world, didn't prepare me for the road up ahead. My wit and my charm only took me so far and when I wasn't getting what he needed, he told me I needed to step things up. My father told me to sleep with some other woman's husband. At that very moment, I knew I was in way over my head. He'd told me to have sex with another man right in front Kemp. I remember looking at Kemp's face that day. He wasn't happy, but he didn't say anything.

It was as though he and my father always had something between the two of them I wasn't aware of. Something I didn't know about. I spoke up for myself. I questioned him, and he simply told me if I couldn't do it to walk away and go home and be a wife…go home and be just like my mother.

I should've listened.

But I hadn't.

I agreed to do it and then I had to do it again and again and again.

But soon, it was all coming to an end.

I loved my father. Even though I knew who he really was, I still loved him. And I knew he loved me too.

But he wasn't the one whose love I was concerned about. His love wasn't the love I needed the most.

The love I wanted and needed more than anything in the world was Kemp's.

And I would do anything to keep it…

Forever.

~***~

LAVA

I heard West calling my name, but I was still standing on the front porch stuck.

Seeing Satin, in some strange way, felt like I'd seen a ghost. It reminded me of what I'd done. Of the fright I'd felt when I thought that I'd killed her.

She looked different, sort of, but even through those fake hazel contacts her eyes told me she was serious about what she'd said to me.

She was serious about doing whatever she had to do to keep Kemp by her side.

She could have him.

She did have him.

I didn't want him.

And seeing her and hearing her words only reminded me of the truth about him. The truth about her.

They killed people. They tricked people. And there was no telling what else they were into.

My heartbeat was racing.

I exhaled loudly, as an attempt to calm down.

Just then, West's friend, George, pulled into the driveway.

They were going fishing.

West still had an attitude with me, and I was sure that he was going to tell George all about it.

"Hey, Lava," George said. I noticed he was wearing his wedding ring again, but I hadn't forgotten about what Thea told me.

He didn't deserve Cheyenne.

But their marriage was his business, so I placed on a fake smile, acknowledged him, and he headed inside.

I heard West yell my name again, so I took a deep breath and headed in behind him.

"What is it?"

"Someone keeps calling your phone," West said.

"Well, did you answer it?"

"Nope."

West grabbed his fishing rods, said goodbye to the kids, and then he and George walked out of the front door without saying another word to me.

I looked out the window at them until they drove away. Finally, I picked up my phone from the coffee table.

It was another strange number that I was sure belonged to Kemp.

I'd told him not to call me.

I'd told him to leave me alone.

The phone started vibrating in my hand again, and I answered it with an attitude.

"Kemp, leave me alone! Like I told you, I want things to go back to how they were…before you came back and…"

"This isn't Kemp," he said. "Lava, this is…"

~***~

"You'll never believe who I just saw!" Thea yelled at me, as she got out her car, holding Baby Fiona just any ole kind of way.

I waited for her to reach the porch. Once she sat down, I asked her.

"Who?"

"Tokyo."

Hearing her name somehow knocked the wind out of me.

I'd never been sure what I would do if I ever saw her again. Though Kemp told me she was alive, in the back of my mind, I thought he was lying.

I thought that she was dead.

"Where?"

"At the store, right down the street from your mama's house. My mama was over there, and she'd watched the baby for me last night. I went to pick her up, and when I was passing back through, I saw Tokyo at the store. She was talking to Drea."

"Drea? My sister?"

"Duh, bitch! Drea was all in her face too! She was pointing and all of this and that. I'm assuming she was going off about what she'd done to you, but I didn't stop. I wanted to, but I know me, and Tokyo and I would've been out there fighting like cats and dogs. I couldn't have that. Not with my baby in the car. Besides, looks like Drea had it covered."

Hurriedly, I called Drea, but she didn't answer.

She never answers her damn phone!

She was always busy and always distant. Once her husband died, she was even worse.

She'd left her job she'd been at for years, and she'd disappeared for months. She'd only told mama she was leaving for a while so no one would be worried. And for a long time, she was just gone.

We'd all tried to call her here and there, but she would never pick up her phone. And then one day she just showed up. A few months after that she told us she was getting married.

Maybe she was going through some kind of mid-life crisis or simply just mourning the death of her husband in her own way.

She'd found him dead in their bed, according to what mama had told us. He never woke up from going to sleep the night before.

Drea also told mama that he'd been battling cancer for quite some time, but she'd never said a word to any of us about it. She'd been dealing with it and taking care of him all on her own.

And then after finding him dead, she had him cremated. No funeral. No family gathering. Nothing. She handled it all by herself. And then she just disappeared.

I called her again.

When she didn't answer, I texted her.

"I wonder what was said."

"Girl, me too. Whatever was said, it looked like the whole thing was heated. Shit, hopefully they didn't start fighting and end up in jail. It sure looked like it was headed in that direction."

I doubted Drea had hit her unless she had to.

She'd walked away from her old position, but she'd found another one and was back to practicing law, so she wouldn't just assault her. I was sure of it. But she would curse her the hell out on my behalf.

"I always wondered what I would do if I saw her again."

"Hopefully, you'll beat the shit out of her," Thea said.

"If she's in town, I wonder if she has plans on trying to get in contact with West," I said to her. Uninvited, worry entered my body.

West and I were already going through it, so I didn't even want to imagine how he would respond if Tokyo reached out to him.

"She better not start no shit again! I'm here this time around and I will fuck her up without thinking twice about it!"

I was still trying to get my thoughts together.

"What's going on with everyone just popping up?"

"Oh, Kemp popped up again?"

"No, but his wife did."

Thea's eyes got as big as golf balls.

"Satin came over here the other day, and she sounded just like me from a year ago. She told me to stay the hell away from Kemp."

Thea smirked.

"I couldn't believe he told her that we—"

"Damn, why would he tell her that?"

I shrugged. "I don't know. But she was pissed! She threatened me, and I could barely say a word. I don't know if it was shock that she was standing right there in front of me or if it was because West was inside, and I couldn't cause a scene because I didn't want him to find out. I barely said anything."

"Lava, don't tell me that you let that woman punk you," Thea laughed.

"Fuck you, Thea. She didn't punk me. I was just…"

It was quiet for a while.

"Well, good thing you don't plan on seeing Kemp again. Right? We don't need any more drama! You need to be focusing on you and West, especially with Tokyo's ass lurking around here. I know Kemp is…Kemp. But West is your reality. If you ask me, all of you should've had just one big ass orgy and called it a day. It's just too much."

Thea was right.

It was all just too much.

I couldn't take back my recent rendezvous with Kemp, but I vowed it would never happen again.

I convinced Thea to ride with me to change my phone number, drop the kids off at mama's, and then to pick out something sexy to wear for West later that night.

Once I was back home, I cooked West's favorite food, fried pork chops, and then I cleaned. I noticed it was getting late, so I called West to see when he would be coming home.

He didn't pick up his phone.

I called him over and over again, until finally, I ate alone. Hours went by and still wearing the overpriced lingerie, after calling him one last time, I got into our bed.

It was after midnight when I turned out the bedroom light and swallowed the lump in my throat.

I already knew he wasn't going to come home.

Oh God.

Is he with *her*?

~***~

SATIN

"I'm coming!"

I knew it was Dedrick at the door.

He was the only other person who knew where I lived besides Kemp, and Kemp wouldn't come over unless he absolutely had to. I always went to his apartment once all of this with Dedrick started. And besides, Kemp had a key.

It had been about two weeks since I'd heard from Dedrick and since his wife and I had gotten into it at the hotel.

Kemp had been texting me, telling me he was still following him. As far as he could tell, they were still together and appeared to be working out their marriage.

Kemp was still planning to kill him though.

He said even if the affair didn't come out and ruin him, my father still wanted him dead and out of the way.

I opened the door.

Dedrick looked at me with a spark in his eyes.

A blind man could see he'd missed me.

"I would've came sooner—"

I walked away from the door, allowing him to follow me.

Dedrick closed the door behind him then joined me on the couch.

"So, you and Carla…"

"We're divorcing…silently."

I stared at him.

"We haven't been happy for a long time. Her catching you there was the final straw. Marrying her was just…anyway, divorce is for the best."

"And she isn't trying to make you look bad?"

"No. We'll be staying in the same house until it's done. The hotel staff all signed a few things. No one will say a word about that day. But that's not why I'm here."

"Then why are you here?"

Dedrick touched my hand.

"Get out."

I looked at him confused.

"What?"

"Get out," he repeated.

"Get out of where?"

Dedrick exhaled. "Out of here. Out of everything. Out of the country. Just get out."

I moved my hand away from him.

What is he talking about?

"I know who you are—Satin. And I know about Kemp."

I jumped to my feet.

"What? What did you say?"

"I know who you are, Satin. We've been tracking your father for years, and we are about to make our move. Get out," he said sternly, standing in front of me.

My mouth fell open and I struggled to close it.

"Working for Homeland Security is part of my cover. I took on the position to get close to a few dirty government officials that are inside and tied to your father. I've been undercover for years. And finally, we are about to make our move. Did you know your father was born here? A U.S. Citizen? He was born in Maryland. His mother and father were here in the States, for whatever reason, before going back to Egypt. Honestly, I think they were what you and Kemp are today. But once your father came into the picture, they headed back and started getting others to do their dirty work for them."

Really?

My grandparents never mentioned ever coming to America. And remembering my grandmother, she wouldn't have hurt a fly. Dedrick's thoughts of them doing what Kemp and I do were probably wrong. But that wasn't the problem at hand.

Him knowing about everything was.

"Satin, your father is connected to everything bad, everything that's wrong, and it isn't just our government that wants him stopped. He has more enemies in his own backyard than he thinks. We're working together to take him and his whole operation down. And the time is coming...soon."

I was frozen.

I had so much to say, but I couldn't seem to get it out.

My father?

Dedrick?

What?

"After the hotel blow up, I was ordered to stay away from you by my superiors. I was never supposed to take things to this level with you. Even my wife has no idea what I've been up to all of these years. When I met her, I was already undercover. I knew exactly who you were when I saw you. You changed your hair and your eyes, but I'd stared at your photos plenty of times. What man wouldn't?

When I saw you at the party, I knew something was in play. I wondered why you were there. I wanted to know what you were up to. So, when I saw you again at the store that day, I approached you. You are the daughter of the very man I've been working for years to take down. But I'm guessing you are here for a reason too."

If only he knew, he only approached me because I'd wanted him to. If only he knew he was the target.

"We know all about your father's organization. We know about the money, the murders, the connections. We know you play some kind of part in it all, but you're not the big fish. You don't get your hands dirty. You don't hurt or kill anyone. But your husband does. And, Satin, he's going down too."

Hearing that, I found the strength to speak.

"Nothing is going to happen to Kemp!"

"Kemp is going to jail, Satin. And so is your father. And if you don't get out of here, right now, you probably will too. I won't be able to control them or protect you. They will arrest you. They will assume you are just as guilty as the rest of them. They will try to get what they can out of you and then you'll be thrown into a cage just like everyone else. But you aren't like them. I've gotten to know you. You may do some things I don't know about, but you're harmless. I know you aren't like them."

"But I am. I'm just like them! I knew what they were doing! I played my part. I served my purpose!"

"But you didn't kill anyone. You were doing what you had been trained and groomed to do. Now, you can get out. Go, Satin. Wherever your husband is, we'll find him. We've been watching your apartment, periodically. I'd set up someone to watch it whenever I wasn't coming over. Why haven't we seen Kemp? From what we know, usually you two are in the same area and he's never too far. So, if he hasn't been around here where is he? Wherever he is, when he's caught, he will spend the rest of his life in prison. So, Satin, please. Just go."

Dedrick tried to touch me, but I moved away from him.

I couldn't believe everything he'd just said to me.

"So, you're not Homeland Security?"

"I'm a little bit of everything. All you need to know is I work for the man in charge and pretty damn determined to bring your father's reign to an end."

He waited for me to comment.

I didn't so he continued.

"I have feelings for you. I'm not supposed to be here. And I tried not to be. My intentions were all bad when I approached you that day. But getting to know you, somehow, made them something else. I'm here because I care. I'm here because I want to save you. Get out of town, Satin. Get out of sight. Get out the country and never look back. Don't ever look back."

Finally, Dedrick walked towards the door. "And you can't take Kemp with you. They'll never stop looking for him and you if you do. They want your father. They want Kemp. But they'll take you too. As long as they have him, they won't care about you. Leave. Go. Alone." Dedrick opened the front door. "Goodbye, Satin. And good luck." He gave me a half smile. As soon as the door closed, I picked up my cell phone.

This couldn't be happening!

They couldn't have my father!

And they damn sure couldn't have my husband!

What am I going to do?

Oh God, what am I going to do?

~***~

KEMP

I pulled the trigger.

That fool Dedrick dropped to the ground.

Dogs started to bark just as I hit the gas, speeding in the opposite direction.

I'd been sitting across the street from his house for hours. Waiting for him to come home. Waiting to kill him.

Satin told me what he'd said.

She told me he knew everything.

The truth about us and who we were.

And he told her that her father's operation was about to come tumbling down.

We would be long gone before it did.

"It's done," I said into the phone.

Satin's father didn't ask any questions. He knew what I meant. He knew I'd done just what he'd asked me to do.

We both hung up.

Satin wanted to tell him what she told me, but I'd convinced her to wait. She'd said Dedrick implied some people close to her father were working against him, so I told her it wouldn't be smart to tell him just yet. I didn't want whoever the snake was to alarm Dedrick and his crew, so I told her as soon as we were on a plane we would warn him to do the same.

I lied.

I had no plans on telling Pops anything until Satin and I were both long gone, and safe.

I was sure Pops was prepared for this.

And no matter what Dedrick said, if they had him, they had it all. Satin's father ordered the hits, but he'd never pulled a trigger, or killed anyone at all.

His hands were clean.

Mine were dirty.

When push comes to shove, I couldn't be sure if Pops would try to save both of our asses or just his.

He had some of the best lawyers that had ever stepped foot inside a courtroom on his team, and I would be a fool to think they couldn't get him out of whatever was ahead. I would be a fool to think they wouldn't try to put it all on me.

Satin couldn't say for sure what Dedrick and his crew knew, but she believed it was quite a bit. The way I saw it, someone would have to take the fall.

And though I had a lot of connections, most of them—all of them were because of Pops.

And if they had to choose…

I loved my father-in-law, but he would have to deal with getting out of this all on his own.

Satin's safety and freedom came first.

Period.

Satin and I were scheduled to be on a plane in the next thirty minutes. Glancing at the clock, she should be in a wig, and half way to the airport by now.

And I was on my way.

Earlier that day, I'd had her to text Dedrick and tell him that she was taking his advice and to ask him not to have anyone watching her apartment. He'd said okay. Even though he'd had Satin's apartment being watched here and there, I wasn't surprised they hadn't spotted me. Though I'd been living right across the parking lot the whole time, I was always careful. I never went to Satin's place anymore and most of the time I parked behind my apartment building and went in and out of my back door.

For now, they didn't know where I was so getting on a plane for me shouldn't be a problem. I'd just wanted to make sure Satin wasn't followed.

We were headed for the Cayman Islands but now that I knew they would be looking for us we wouldn't stay there. Most likely we would settle somewhere in the heart of South America. I'd met a connection there years ago that I knew Pops didn't know about. He'd shared some information with me about disappearing in South America, and I had plans to check it out.

I just had to get us away from here first.

From one of my other phones, I tried calling Lava one last time. She'd changed her phone number, but I'd gotten the new one. I hadn't bothered to call it until now.

Satin told me she'd gone to see her.

She even told me she threatened her.

I'd wanted to apologize to her.

I'd wanted to…

Once it went to her voicemail, I tossed the phone out of the window.

Goodbye, Lava.

As of right now, Satin was my main and only concern.

I raced towards the airport.

From my other phone, the one that only Satin's number was in, I called her to see if she was already at the airport, but she didn't pick up

I would do anything to keep her out of prison which was why I knew they had to catch the big fish.

Pops.

He would roll over on me as soon as they got him in the interrogation room, but he would never mention Satin.

And by the time he put it all on me, Satin and I would be somewhere being called Pablo and Maria.

I called Satin again.

"Come on, baby, answer the phone."

A mile from the airport, I confirmed the time on our plane tickets that had been purchased under another fake identity that I'd created years ago and never shared with anyone else.

You know, just in case.

Just in case this day ever came.

I glanced at the clock. We had about fifteen minutes before our plane was scheduled to be in the air, so I called her again.

Still she didn't pick up.

What the fuck?

I called her again.

Still, no answer.

Something was wrong.

She knew I would've been calling. She knew we were on a schedule and I would be checking in to make sure she was at the airport. She would've answered her phone. If she could. She wouldn't have missed my calls.

I made a U-turn, racing back towards Satin's apartment.

I passed back by Dedrick's house just to scope out the scene, only to find there wasn't one.

No police officers. No media coverage. Nothing.

I was sure I'd shot him.

I never miss.

I'd watched him go down to the ground.

But he was gone. And so was his car.

Fuck!

Minutes later I reached Satin's apartment. I scanned the parking lot for her car. It was still there. I circled around the parking lot three times until I was sure that I didn't see any unmarked police cars then I got out of my car.

Head down, I walked towards her apartment. The closer I got, I could see her front door was cracked open.

"Satin!"

I yelled for her as I entered the apartment. Shit was all over the place. As though there had been some type of scuffle.

"Satin! Satin! Satin!"

But she didn't answer.

I searched every room, but she wasn't there.

She wasn't anywhere.

My wife…my partner in crime…

Was gone.

****

Chapter FIVE

LAVA

"I'll be gone all day. I'm helping George and Cheyenne move into their new house," West said.

"They finally sold the other one?"

"Yeah."

West and I were still in a dry place.

We'd gone to a counseling session, and he'd been brutally honest. He told the counselor he caught me masturbating while thinking about another man, and it'd made him feel like all of the counseling had been a waste of time. He said that he could barely look at me and that he didn't want to touch me.

I'd shot back by saying I would've never known Kemp, in that way if it had not been for him and his affair with Tokyo.

And that only made things worse.

By the end of the session, I was in tears, begging West to forgive me.

He'd said no.

And he still wouldn't tell me where he'd been that night he hadn't come home. My thoughts were all over the place.

West walked out the front door, and I watched him from the window.

I hadn't told him Tokyo was back in town. Well, at least she had been, and he hadn't mentioned her. I couldn't help but wonder if she'd reached out to him.

Finally, after days of calling her, I'd finally been able to get Drea on the phone.

I told her Thea saw her and Tokyo arguing at a store and asked her what happened.

Drea said her and Tokyo had gotten into it over what she'd done to me, but that the conversation hadn't been much of anything to tell. She said she confronted her, and Tokyo hadn't tried to deny it. Drea said she told her that she'd better not even think about coming anywhere near me or my husband again.

Tokyo said she wouldn't.

According to Drea, Tokyo didn't seem to be interested in West at all.

Maybe she wasn't.

Or maybe she was playing her, just like she'd played me for all those years.

Nevertheless, my guard was up and I was trying my best to fix my mess, hoping Tokyo wouldn't be able to weasel her way back into our lives and take my husband away from me again.

My insecurities made me wonder if West was really going to help George move or if he was sneaking off to be with her.

Or someone else.

With the kids laughing and running around the house, I made myself a cup of tea then headed outside to sit on the front porch.

It was a beautiful Saturday, and it would've been the perfect day to do something as a family. But West couldn't have gotten out of the house and away from me fast enough.

I sat there.

Enjoying the breeze and scenery. Trying to sort through my thoughts and feelings, and somehow, I ended up on memory lane…

And guess what memories were waiting for me?

The ones that included times and conversation with Kemp. Thinking back, I'd told Kemp things I'd never told anyone before.

He just had this way of pulling out my most intimate thoughts, secrets, and desires. I'd told him everything except my dirty little secret involved Drea's dead husband and my virginity.

But to be honest, I'd thought about telling him that too. It would've felt good to finally tell someone and get it off of my chest. But some things were better left unsaid, especially now since he was dead.

I looked at the car pulling into my driveway.

It was my sister Declora.

She and I were closest in age and had been closer when we were younger. With her being a single mom and a career woman, over the years, we grew further and further apart.

"Hey chica," she said to me.

She walked up the porch steps and kissed my cheek.

"What brings you by? I can't believe you're here."

I could tell something was wrong.

"I need to ask you something. I wasn't sure who to ask, but… We both know how friendly our sister, Janay, is with her vagina."

Uh oh.

"I mean, she's had a lot of guy friends. We all know that," Declora continued. "But what if one of her guys from a *long* time ago happens to be a really great guy…and I've been seeing him?"

Ahh, hell!

She looked at me and waited for me to respond. I couldn't open my mouth. Not just yet.

"They dated almost ten years ago for about three months. Rocky. Do you remember him?"

I tried to put his face with a name, but Janay had been with a lot of men. Honestly, I couldn't be sure if Janay would even remember him.

"I didn't remember him either but when I started talking about my sisters he asked more questions about Janay, and we discovered that it was one in the same. He said he'd come to a cookout that had at mama and daddy's house, but I couldn't remember. Anyway, I should've cut the conversation short right then and there, but I didn't. And now, I'm not sure if I want to. I know he dated my sister and they had sex, but more than likely he'd meant nothing to her. She didn't mean anything to him either, but he's starting to mean a whole lot to me. I think he is the one. I think he's the man I've been waiting on all of this time. I just hadn't expected *the one* to have been with one of my sisters."

Declora was a successful, hardworking mommy of three. She didn't need a man for anything, and she wasn't one of those women who was always out here looking for love or attention. She was fine making her own money and raising her kids all by herself. If this man, Rocky, had her attention, he must be pretty damn awesome.

"I'm not sure what to do. I haven't had sex with him. *Yet*. But I want to. I just don't want to hurt or upset Janay."

Well I'd slept with one of our sister's men before, so I was probably the wrong one to be giving her advice about this.

"Ask her."

Declora looked at me.

"Ask her?"

"Ask her if she'll have a problem with you dating someone she used to date…screw. That's the only thing that I can think of."

"It's nasty I even want to date him, right? I mean, she's my sister, and they had sex."

"He could've had sex with worse," I shrugged. "Prostitutes, a man…you never know these days."

Declora shook her head. "So, you think Janay…"

"Oh, she's going to make a big deal out of it. We know how she is. But still, tell her. Ask her. Especially if you really think there could be something real between the two of you."

"I do."

"Well, there you have it."

Declora was quiet for a moment.

I admired her.

Of all my sisters, though Drea had been just a little more successful than she was, if I'd had to choose, I would want to be like Declora.

She just had this calmness and beauty about her. She was different, unique, and in that moment, I realized how much I missed her.

"I guess I should get it out the way as soon as possible. I want to bring him to the wedding."

That's right.

Drea's wedding would be here soon.

"Have you met the groom?"

"Only twice. You?"

"Twice for me too. Who is he? She just popped up after keeping to herself for a few months. All of a sudden, she's marrying someone else."

"They used to work together, I think. And yes, I think she's moving way too fast. I think she just misses Sean.

Hell, they'd been together forever. Since we were in our teens," Declora said.

I didn't respond.

The mentioning of Sean's name made me feel guilty.

But I understood what Declora was saying.

Drea had him cremated so fast, and from what mama had told us, his family had gotten a little upset. Mama had to be the one to tell them the bad news. And then Drea was just gone. None of us had seen her mourn. And when she came back, she acted as though nothing was wrong. As though her husband hadn't recently died. She quickly found a new job, and somewhere along the way, she ended up with a new fiancé too.

"Do you think she was seeing him before Sean died?"

"I don't know. The thought did cross my mind though. But I don't know about that. Drea loved Sean. I just can't see her having an affair."

"Most people don't see a lot of things about people. It doesn't mean that it isn't there."

I shrugged.

"Well, I got my dress. And this bachelorette party is next week so I'll be there. If it all blows up in her face, I'll be there for that too."

"Me too. That's what sisters are for." Declora said a few more words then she said that she had to go and she would see me later.

Once she drove away, I couldn't help but wonder how it all was going to turn out. I already knew Janay was going to make a big deal about it, and in the end, Declora was going to end up with a broken heart.

But when it came down to love, I guess anything was worth a shot.

~***~

"So, Ying is finally coming home?"

Thea exhaled. "Yes! I was starting to think he was trying to dip out on a bitch or something," Thea laughed.

Ying did seem to be skeptical about returning to the States. Thea had moved back into their old house and had everything ready for him, but he'd kept delaying his trip back home.

"He should be home, for sure, the beginning of next week. They had to take his mother to the hospital again, so I'm pretty sure that lit a fire under his ass. That man loves his little ugly ass mama. Hell, he should've been trying to hurry up and get home to me and his daughter. But whatever works. Whatever gets his ass here!"

Ying being involved in the money scandal had surprised me. But learning he'd known someone who could get him in contact with someone like Kemp surprised me even more.

Speaking of Kemp, he was involved with something that was about to come crashing down on him. Or maybe things already had.

A while back, before I'd changed my phone number, I'd gotten a strange phone call from a man who was asking me about him.

I don't know who he was, but he knew my name.

He'd given me a name, but I was pretty sure that it was a fake because he'd stuttered while saying it. But he'd asked me if I'd seen or spoken to Kemp.

I'd said not recently and that I'd asked Kemp not to contact me again. When I'd tried to ask the man on the phone a question, he simply hung up.

I'd thought about calling and telling Kemp that day, but I hadn't. He wasn't my problem, and I didn't want to be caught up in whatever it was he was involved it.

I didn't need any more problems, especially not any legal ones. So, I didn't warn him someone was asking about him. I just simply let it be.

Especially with his wife on the prowl.

She could have her husband, and all the things that came with him. I was the least of her worries or concerns. I didn't have time to be her husband's mistress. After all, I was too busy making sure that my husband didn't find his way back to his.

~***~

SATIN

"Help me! Please… Somebody, please… Help me!"

KEMP

"Where the fuck is she?"

I had the gun at the back of Dedrick's head.

"Kemp."

"I know my motherfucking name! Now where is Satin? Where the fuck is my wife?"

It was obvious somebody had taken her.

The scene told it all.

She'd fought back. Pillows were all over the place. A chair was kicked over and papers were all over the floor. Her bag was half packed, her phone was left behind, and so was her purse.

Music was still on and so was the shower.

The door was unlocked so that meant she'd opened the door.

And she wouldn't have opened it for anyone but Dedrick.

"Where is she?"

"Who?"

I removed the safety from my gun. At the clicking sound, he spoke again.

"The last time I saw Satin was days, maybe even a week ago. At her apartment. I'm assuming you know where that is. That is the last time I saw her. Since that day, I haven't spoken to her again. Other than a text message. That's all."

"Don't fuck with me!"

Dedrick turned around to face me.

"You shot me the other day, didn't you?" he asked.

Yeah. I knew I hadn't missed.

"I was wearing a vest. I had a feeling that anything could happen once I told Satin the truth. Once I told her who I really was and that we were coming for you."

"Where is she?"

"Like I told you, I don't know. The last time I saw her, she was at home. Maybe she left. Maybe she got the hell out of dodge like I told her to. Maybe she left without you."

He chuckled, like the shit was funny.

"Trust me, she didn't leave without me. Someone took her. Something happened to her. She's missing."

"Look, *if* she's missing, I didn't have anything to do with it and neither did the men that I work for or with. They want her to spend the rest of her life in a cell. I wanted her to get away. Looks like she did."

Dedrick turned his back to me as though he wasn't afraid of me pulling the trigger.

I wanted to put one in the back of his head, right then and there, but on a hunch, I decided I would let him live.

For now.

I had a feeling he knew more than what he was telling me. I had a feeling he was going to lead me to Satin.

Saying nothing else, with my gun still in my hand, I struck out running in the opposite direction.

Satin wouldn't leave without me.

No matter what she was tripping about concerning Lava, she wouldn't go anywhere without me.

At least, not willingly.

Someone took her from me.

I'd called Pops.

I told him Dedrick was still alive, but I didn't tell him Satin was missing.

He'd told me to wait awhile before making another attempt on Dedrick, but he seemed to be clueless about the things Dedrick had told Satin. He didn't have a clue that shit was about to hit the fan.

Unless it was all for show.

I've always had trust issues, but now, more than ever.

With Satin missing, I was really tripping.

I didn't know what to think.

Maybe Pops already knew what was about to take place. Maybe he already knew Satin was missing. She could've told him, warned him, even though I told her not to. Maybe he took her to keep her safe and left me to fend for myself.

I'd parked about a block away from Dedrick's house. I didn't stop running until I reached my car.

Now that Dedrick knew I was in town, I knew I would have to really watch my back. In all honesty, I knew I needed to get the hell out of here, but I couldn't leave.

Not without Satin.

I'd gone through Satin's apartment over and over again, looking for something that could have been left behind. Looking for something that might tell me where she was or tell me who took her.

Nothing.

Dedrick was my initial thought, but I was an expert at reading people. Just from the tone of his voice and how it slightly cracked when he responded to my questions about her, I knew he hadn't taken her.

I knew he hadn't even known she was missing.

But she was.

And someone had her.

Since he was trying to put me in prison, I was going to have to lay low, off his radar, and search for Satin at the same time.

I couldn't end up in jail without finding her. And I couldn't disappear and leave her.

The thought to tell Pops what was going on, just to see, kept crossing my mind. Maybe he could see something I couldn't. But for some reason, I kept hearing a voice in my head, telling me not to trust him, and so, I didn't.

I had to figure this out all on my own.

Maybe I hadn't seen something that was already there.

I kept my eyes on the road as I drove, but my mind was on Satin.

We'd talked about what Dedrick said to her, constantly, before coming up with a plan to leave. She told me Dedrick had made it clear whatever the police, or government, or whoever was planning it was coming soon. Real soon.

She said he kept bringing up my name and that he told her if they had both me and Pops then they wouldn't care if they didn't have her.

Maybe she was trying to save herself.

Nah.

She worked with us, but she didn't know how to move like I moved. She wouldn't be able to hide, forever, without me. Not without my help.

I started to think further back.

Lava.

She'd gone to see Lava and threatened her.

She'd told me exactly what she'd said to her.

Lava had tried to kill Satin once.

Would she try again?

No.

Lava didn't want me. She had no reason to come after Satin. No reason to take her from me.

I drove towards Satin's apartment.

From a distance, I could see the blue lights in front of Satin's apartment building, so I rode past and kept driving around in circles. On my way back around, for maybe the fifth time, I saw Dedrick pull up, get out of his car, and walk into the apartment building.

He believed me.

He was going to see if Satin was really missing, and he'd probably been hoping to find me there in the process.

Dedrick was about to make his move.

On Pops.

And on me, if he can catch me.

I had to disappear but not without my baby.

Without Satin, I wasn't going anywhere.

~***~

LAVA

"Are you going to the bachelorette party?"

Drea was set to get married in two weeks. The bachelorette party was that night.

"Girl, you already know I am! With Ying already on the plane coming home, I may as well have some fun while I still can." Thea was all smiles. "There's gonna be strippers there, right?" she confirmed.

"Um huh."

"Good! Wherever the dicks are, so shall I be!" she yelled with a laugh as she walked out of the front door to go home and get dressed.

Shortly afterwards, West walked in.

"What were the kids doing?"

"Running around when I left."

West had taken the kids to my parents for the weekend.

All the girls were gearing up to have a night full of fun with Drea.

Recently, she'd invited us all out to dinner.

She'd told us once her and Boris, her fiancé, were married, they would be moving. Both had taken jobs at a new firm in Atlanta, and they were scheduled to start working right after their honeymoon.

It seemed as though she was running again, but at least she was telling everyone this time instead of just disappearing like she had before.

She'd wanted to confirm she was happy and, for the first time, she answered all our questions about him.

Drea used to be a District Attorney before just walking away from it, and he, Boris, had worked with her for over six years. She said he'd always had a thing for her, but she'd been married. Once she came back, she said she called him and things went from there.

They agreed that they knew each other pretty well and neither of them wanted to waste time. She said she just wanted to get married and move on.

And that's exactly what she was doing.

Our mother didn't seem convinced, but Drea assured her she was happy and she'd wanted to have another chance at happily ever after.

And so, the wedding was on.

That night we all sat around and made jokes with Drea and her new beau…until the night took a turn for the worst.

My sister, Declora, somewhat changed the energy in the room when she decided to tell Janay she was seeing one of her exes. Honestly, the conversation went better than expected, but there was still a big blow up and a whole lot of tension.

Janay wasn't happy about the idea.

She couldn't understand why Declora wanted someone she'd already been with.

Declora then told Janay she loved him.

Janay laughed at her, and things got a little wild for a few minutes. Finally, Declora said she would never let a man come between her and her sister. She told Janay if she had a problem with it she wouldn't see him again.

But surprisingly, by the end of the conversation, Janay gave Declora her blessing with somewhat of a warning.

She told Declora she would see why she stopped fooling around with him sooner or later.

I couldn't wait to find out what she'd meant by that.

"What time are you leaving tonight?" West asked.

I stood up and walked over to him.

He was still acting being distant with me, but slowly, he was getting over catching me fingering myself to thoughts of Kemp.

I pushed West towards the wall.

"What?" he asked.

Slowly, I made my way down to my knees in front of him.

"Get up, Lava," West demanded.

"Nope."

I started to undo his belt.

"Stop," he hissed.

"Make me," I teased. He was already standing at attention, so I knew he didn't mean a word that he was saying.

He wanted me. He wanted it.

I exposed him and I didn't hesitate to place him inside my mouth.

West cooed.

I was tired of us being on bad terms. I just wanted it to be over. I wanted us to make up. Hell, I wanted us to have sex. It had been way too long. Whether he wanted to or not, he was going to give me some…and damn it, he was going to like it!

Channeling my inner freak, I sucked and slurped him into submission. He tried to fight it, but he couldn't. Finally, he surrendered and allowed me to have my way with him. And before I knew it, West and I were rolling around all over the living floor, making love like we'd never made love before.

"Wow," West breathed, all of thirty minutes later once we were done.

"Baby, I'm sorry. I don't know why, but…"

"Just let it go, Lava," he said.

I took a deep breath. "Okay."

I tried to start a conversation, but West interrupted me and invited me to take a shower with him which led to us making love again.

Before I knew it, I was running behind, and it was time to go.

Janay was hosting the bachelorette party, so I knew it was going to be exciting and outrageous. I was expecting a lot of alcohol, wild and crazy games, and chocolate, sexy male strippers. And I, for one, just couldn't wait!

With a text message from Thea, I glanced back at West settled in bed watching T.V. just as I headed out our bedroom.

"I love you." I looked back at him.

"I love you too, Lava."

I smiled at him and damn near ran out of the front door. Thea was already outside. Immediately, she got out of her car, so she could get into mine.

"Damn! Meow!" she sounded. "Come here, girl, let me scratch that kitty cat." Thea laughed.

We'd been instructed to dress up in a sexy costume. I'd decided to be a cat.

"Honey, trust me, West gonna try and get you pregnant when you get back home," Thea said once we were settled inside of my jeep.

I stared at her.

"And who in the hell are you supposed to be? *Chucky's* side chick?"

Thea looked like she was going to a funeral.

"Hell, I'll be anything you want me to be. Just let me be great, um-kay?"

We shared a chuckle then were finally on our way.

We arrived at Janay's to find a packed house.

I didn't even know Drea knew so many people. I concluded most of the women were probably Janay's friends she'd invited over just for the fun.

Once we were inside, I immediately noticed Drea dressed up as a sexy angel. She had on a halo with wings, but she was also wearing an all-white bustier, white fishnet stockings and a pair of six-inch heels.

She noticed us and headed in our direction.

"Hey, sissy!" she yelled as she kissed me on the cheek. "Janay really outdid herself! Taste this!"

She handed me a drink.

"Ummm, that's good as hell!"

Thea took the drink out my hand, tasted it, then asked Drea to take her to get one.

I headed to find Declora and Janay.

They were standing beside each other at a table, but I could tell all the way from across the room Janay was still in her feelings. Declora was smiling from ear to ear, but Janay kept looking back at her and secretly rolling her eyes.

They both greeted me before Janay gave me a nametag. Shortly afterwards, the fun began.

For the next hour or so, we laughed, danced, and everything in between. We even did freak-in-the-sheets karaoke. And then the *chocolate* came in.

"Yeeeeahhh, baby!" Janay yelled.

Three men dressed as cops came into the center of the living room.

"Whoooo!"

I was drunk as hell.

How in the hell was Thea and I going to get home?

The men began to undress, and all the ladies started to go crazy.

One of them grabbed Drea, and she took a seat in the chair that had been placed there for her.

I took out my phone and attempted to take pictures.

"I'm fucking one of them tonight," I heard Thea say.

"What?"

"Nothing. That was just my horny pussy talking. *She* didn't mean it," she said, taking a sip of her drink.

Giggling together, we enjoyed the show. After a few minutes, I told her I was going to go outside to get some fresh air.

I felt like a roasting turkey until I stepped onto the porch.

The cool breeze slapped me in my face, causing me to close my eyes but once I opened them the sight of her caused me to jump.

Tokyo?

She was standing there on the sidewalk, looking towards the house.

She noticed me, noticing her, but she didn't move.

What the hell is she doing here?

It was dark, but I could tell she was looking right at me.

Suddenly, all the angry I'd felt towards her came rushing back to me at once.

My mind was racing. I was so drunk I could barely find the steps to walk down them. I feared she might get the best of me if I approached her, so I changed my mind about running in her direction. I simply held onto the railing of the steps instead.

For a second, it looked as though she was going to take a step towards me but then...

Wait...is that...

Is that a baby crying?

Whose baby is that?

Tokyo heard it and turned to run towards a car that was parked across the street. She hoped into it, and without even turning on her lights, she sped away.

Wait a minute... Tokyo had a baby?

I thought she couldn't have kids.

That's what she'd said.

That's what her ex-husband had said.

Was it a lie?

It was definitely a baby in her car. I'd heard it loud in clear.

Abruptly, fear started to consume me.

Was it West's?

Had Tokyo had a baby by my husband?

Is that why she'd come back?

Is that why she was here?

I felt the urge to throw up, but I didn't. Instead, I hurried back into the house. I stepped inside just in time to find all hell breaking loose.

"You said you didn't care!"

"I don't! But as my sister you should've never crossed that line in the first place!"

I knew it was coming!

I was just hoping it would be in private and not in front of people we barely even knew. And definitely not at a bachelorette party.

Janay and Declora were arguing about Rocky—again.

Thea was holding Janay by the arm, and Drea was standing in front of Declora.

"The two of you weren't even serious! It was just sex!"

"And I'm sure it's just sex for him with you too!"

"Wrong! We've never had sex, thank you! We've been seeing each other for months, and he's never gotten the goods!"

Janay laughed. "Oh, honey, don't think that it has anything to do with you! It's because of his limp dick!"

Thea spit out her drink.

"What?" Declora questioned.

"You heard me! His dick don't even get hard unless you play with his *shit*…and I mean that literally! He likes you to suck his dick with one of your fingers going in and out his butthole. That's the only way his shit stands up!"

Everyone was laughing, except for me and Declora.

She looked embarrassed. She looked upset.

"Fuck you, Janay!"

Janay shot a look at her, but Drea started to slur.

"Look now…*look*! Damn it! It's my bachelorette party! I'm getting married! He's just a guy! Janay, you said that you didn't care so just let it go. It wasn't like you were married to the man. Now that would've been a different story. That would've been fucked up," she slurred and took another sip out of her cup.

My heart stopped beating.

"Now, when it happened to me…"

Everyone looked at her in confusion.

What is she talking about?

What does she know?

Drea looked at me and smirked, as I placed my hand on my chest. I already knew what she was about to say. "Lava did it to me. Lava slept with my husband. Didn't you, Lava?"

My mouth opened wide as all heads turned in my direction. And suddenly, all eyes were on me.

If only I could disappear…

****

Chapter SIX

SATIN

It's so dark.

I can't see anything.

Where am I?

Please. Somebody. Help me!

Kemp.

Please find me.

~***~

KEMP

Someone was watching me.

I knew it. I could feel it.

What I didn't know was who it was.

Was it the government? The police?

Or was it someone watching me for Pops?

He'd been asking me about Satin, and eventually, he was going to know something was wrong.

If he didn't know it or suspect it already.

I was looking for her.

On my life I was.

But I couldn't find her.

There hadn't been any sign of her in over a week.

My gut told me that she wasn't dead.

Then where is she?

I checked my surroundings before getting into my car.

I didn't see anyone, but somebody was there.

I drove in a hurry towards Dedrick's house.

I'd been watching him and his wife, constantly, but I hadn't seen anything out the ordinary.

On most days, both went to work, made a few random stops in between, and then came back home.

Except for the days his wife Carla went to therapy, and the days when Dedrick would stop by Satin's apartment or go and meet who I now knew were a few government officials in dark alleys or at abandoned buildings. I'd followed him the other day as he dropped off his car and got into another one. I ran the license plate to find it was registered to the FBI.

I was most likely the topic of discussion.

Dedrick was going by Satin's apartment so my guess was he cared about her and wanted to know if something had really happened to her. He'd told her to leave but I was guessing now he wasn't sure if she had.

He was concerned.

He wasn't a suspect.

But I had my thoughts about his wife.

His wife, Carla, caught Satin having an affair with her husband and now, according to what Satin had told me, they were getting a divorce.

Maybe she wanted revenge. Maybe she'd had someone to do something to Satin or take her.

I parked across the street from their house and opened one of my energy drinks.

I was too paranoid to sleep these days. I sat my gun in the passenger seat just as Dedrick's wife pulled into the driveway. She went inside of the house and about an hour later Dedrick came home. He was talking on his cell phone all the way to the front door. Just as he turned the knob, he hung up.

I settled in.

I picked up my phone a few times, and by instinct, I almost called Satin's number. Then I remembered she was gone and that I had her cell phone.

I tried to remember if we'd ever been away from each other this long. No matter what we had to do, we were never too far from each other. Even when she faked her death, Satin hadn't left Virginia until I bombed the courthouse and went with her.

I always kept her close.

I always knew where she was.

Until now.

It was killing me not knowing where she was or what she was doing. If she was hurting or afraid.

Whoever did this to her, whoever took her, was already dead. They just didn't know it yet.

My mind shifted to the day I fell for her.

She didn't know this, but I didn't truly start loving her until about two years into our marriage.

I was young, and for a while, she was just the woman that had been given to me.

I'd done what was expected of me.

I touched her. I learned to protect her. I pretended to love her. But I didn't actually fall in love with her until one particular day.

Love.

Real love usually hits you by surprise. When you least expect it. It makes falling so much easier.

We'd just finished one of our language lessons. To date, Satin and I spoke six different languages.

That day, her father was being honored for varies things he had his hands in, and we were scheduled to attend.

After we both dressed, Satin told me that she didn't want to go. Instead, she'd wanted to go watch the sunset and drink grape soda.

So, that's what we did.

I sat there in some expensive ass suit and watched her as she ripped the sleeves off a five thousand dollar dress.

She tied the bottom of the dress into a knot, pulled her hair up into a high ponytail, and wiped off her makeup. It was like I was looking at a different person.

She laughed at the look that was on my face then she started to talk to me.

But she talked differently.

She'd spent two years saying and doing all the right things. She'd always been so proper. Always did what she was trained to do as a wife. Always spoke to me with the upmost respect. Never raised her voice at me. Never got upset.

But that day, she stopped pretending.

She wasn't some stuck-up, entitled, millionaire brat.

All that time, she'd just been pretending. She'd been being who they told her be.

As we sat there, she asked me one thing.

She asked me if she could just be herself for a few hours. If she could just be who she wanted to be.

And so, she was.

She talked about everything under the sun. She talked about things I was surprised she knew about. She knew slang, she knew about music and art. She even knew about hip-hop and she cursed. I'd never heard her curse until that day. She amazed me. She impressed me. And then, the exact moment I fell in love with her was when she looked at me and said:

"So, about that little thing you do with your tongue…during sex… Um, yeah, you need to watch some porn or something because I don't like that." She giggled.

I laughed at her and fell for her right then.

I told her to always be honest with me from then on. To always show her true self with me; she never had to hide or fake it again.

And after that day, she didn't.

She opened up, and that's when our marriage really began. Through all the things we were preparing to do, we grew. We lived. We loved.

And then it came time for her to seduce her first mark.

I'll never forget the day Pops sat us down and told us he was sending us into the world to do what he'd trained us to do.

He hadn't wanted Satin to be a part of it all in the beginning, but he knew she would be able to do things that we couldn't do.

He warned Satin there may come a time where she would have to do some things she probably wouldn't want to do.

I don't think either of us knew what he meant, but we soon found out.

Pops needed information on and from a man named Ori. He was Satin's first assignment. He was married, of course, but he was also heavily involved with politics. And he was a murderer. Pops needed bodies, accomplices, or proof of his crimes to blackmail him. I was sent to recruit as my first assignment, but he'd made sure I wasn't too far away to protect her.

We went home for a weekend during the assignment.

Satin told him what she was doing wasn't working. She wasn't getting what he needed from Ori. She didn't know anything about his secrets.

That's when Pops told her she needed to do more. She needed to earn his trust. She needed to be closer to him. She needed to become his weakness. And his mistress. She needed to give herself to him.

And he'd said it right in front of me.

At the time, we'd wanted to make a difference. But I didn't want anyone touching my wife but me.

Still, I didn't speak up.

I didn't fear Pops back then, but what could I do?

I spoke to Satin about it. Though she continued to try to get closer to her *mark* without sex for a while, she finally told me she had to take the next step.

But Dedrick had been her last *step*.

Now all I wanted to do was find her and get her as far away from here, and as far away from Pops as I could.

If only I had a clue...

Beep. Beep. Beep.

Damn. I'd fallen asleep.

I turned off the alarm on my phone and looked towards Dedrick's house. His car was already gone and his wife was coming out of the front door.

She got into her car and I started up mine, pulling out behind her.

I followed her, expecting her to head to work like any other day. Only today, she headed for the highway instead.

Curious, I continued to follow her, keeping my distance while wondering what it was she was up to.

Wondering where she was going or who she was going to see.

We drove for a little while.

What the fuck?

We started to pass signs that said Virginia, and it didn't take me long to realize where we were headed.

Fairfax.

My entire body swelled with anger and suspicion once she took the exit.

The same exit that led me to Lava.

After driving through town and passing Sager Avenue, I knew exactly where she was going.

Dedrick's wife pulled up at West's auto shop, and hastily, she got out the car.

West met her at the door, and she walked inside the shop and disappeared.

What the fuck is she doing here?

~***~

LAVA

"I still can't believe you didn't tell me," Thea complained.

"I didn't tell anyone. I didn't know how to," I said ashamed. "I don't know how Drea found out, and she won't tell me."

The other night, in front of everyone, Drea revealed that she knew I'd had sex with her deceased husband, Sean.

I'd tried to laugh it off and deny it, but Drea told me it was no point. She told me she'd known for a long time, but she wouldn't tell me how she found out.

Obviously, Sean had to tell her or maybe he'd told someone else who told her. Either way, she'd found out. Either way, my secret was out.

I couldn't tell if Drea was angry that night. She was more drunk than anything. In fact, in the middle of my explanation, she'd passed out.

Literally.

The next morning, she didn't even remember saying what she said but once it was brought up she looked at me as though she regretted telling me what she knew.

"And you and Drea?"

I shrugged.

I expected Drea to want details. To scream at me and possibly even want to fight but after she was told what she'd said she didn't want to talk about it. She'd blamed it on a headache and left Janay's house as fast as she could.

I hadn't talked to her since.

I'd wanted to tell her the whole story. That I was young, horny, and stupid. And I wanted to assure her it had happened before they were married. I wanted to tell her my side of the story. My truth. But she hadn't given me the chance.

"Well, she didn't kick you out of the wedding…right?"

"No. She didn't."

"Well maybe she just wants to move on from it. After all, he's dead," Thea shrugged. "And just for the record, you ain't touched *my* Ying, have you?"

I rolled my eyes at Thea. "No. What happened between Sean and I happened when I was young and before they were even married. He was my first, Thea."

She gasped. "What! Sean, your sister's husband, was your first? Like your first-first?"

I nodded. "Yes."

"So, Two-minute Tommy didn't take your virginity?"

"No, he was my second. Sean was my first."

Thea shook her head. "What were you thinking, Lava?"

"I have no idea. I guess I didn't think they would get married. I didn't think he would be around long. It was obvious he was just using her. I thought surely he was as good as dumped once Drea saw his true colors. I hadn't expected her to marry him or to have to see him with my sister for almost twenty-years."

Thea shook her head. "If it's something you need to tell me, go on and tell me so I can beat you up and get it over with."

"Thea…"

"What? I'm serious." She glanced at her phone. She didn't recognize the number, so she didn't answer it. "Are you going to tell West?"

"I probably should before someone else does. We're just now getting back on good terms, so I'm not sure how that's going to work out."

I'd been thinking about that for the past two days.

Whether or not I should tell West what everyone else already knew. I was worried about how he was going to react. I was wondering what he was going to say and how he was going to look at me once I told him the truth.

"Speaking of West, I'd gone outside the night of the party and Tokyo was there."

"Tokyo?"

"Yeah, she was just standing there on the sidewalk."

"For what?"

"She was just standing there. And then…I heard a baby cry."

"A baby? Girl, we were all tore up that night. Are you sure?"

"Yes, because once the baby started crying Tokyo ran towards her car and drove away."

Thea appeared to be in deep thought. Finally, she spoke.

"So...do you think it's her baby? West's baby?"

"She said she couldn't have kids."

"Chile, she lied about every damn thing else! Lord, it's probably West's baby, chile!"

That's what I was afraid of.

I had no idea what I would say or do if Tokyo popped up carrying West's child. She could've been lying. She could've lied to her husband all those years about not being able to get pregnant. Maybe she just couldn't get pregnant by him.

"When you saw her fussing with Drea, did you see a baby?"

"No, but if she left the baby in the car that night she could've had the baby in the car then too. There's no way to be sure," Thea commented. "And who the hell is this that keeps calling my phone?"

Thea screamed hello and then she apologized once she realized it was her mother's new number.

As she talked on the phone, I mentally rehearsed what I was going to say to West about what I'd done to Drea. But no matter what I said, I had the feeling the end result would be the same. My husband would never look at me the same.

~***~

"Kemp? What are you doing here?"

"How does your husband know Carla?"

His hair was messy and all over his head, but somehow, the sight of him still turned me on.

Stop it, Lava!

"Who is Carla?"

Kemp had popped up at my house yet again.

I was nervous. Being in his presence made me nervous. My body and my mind never did what I told it to or what it was supposed to do whenever he was around.

Not to mention, I was also nervous because I didn't know when West would be home. And I damn sure didn't want to have to deal with his wife.

"I don't know Carla. Should I know Carla?"

Kemp stared at me.

"Lava, Satin is missing."

"Missing? What do you mean missing?"

Briefly, Kemp filled me in. He told me how long Satin had been gone. She'd had an affair with Carla's husband, and then Carla and Satin had gotten into a fight, and Satin had gone to jail. He also said the husband Satin had an affair with had decided to divorce his wife. I was pretty sure there was more to the story but instead of telling all the backstory he jumped to the day Satin went missing, and from there, he jumped to the day before when he'd followed the wife to West's auto shop.

Kemp was sure it wasn't just a coincidence. He told me Carla lived in Washington and that's where he and Satin had been living as well. That's why I hadn't seen them around, except when they both just decided to pop up.

"What does Carla coming here to see West have to do with anything?"

"I don't know. That's what I'm trying to figure out."

"Surely, you don't think West has anything to do with Satin being missing. And he hasn't mentioned anything about a Carla to me."

I couldn't help but wonder why she'd gone to see him too. Surely, she hadn't come from Washington to Virginia just to have her car worked on at his shop.

"I have a feeling her visit has something to do with Satin. And maybe even your husband."

I folded my arms across my chest.

"That's just the thing. Why would it have something to do with West? He wasn't the one sleeping with Satin, remember? I was wrong. It was his friend George as you know. So why would West know anything about where Satin is? Or that she's missing? Why would you think he could possibly be involved with whatever this Carla chick may or may not have done?"

"I don't know. But I'll find out."

I could see the worry in his eyes.

In that moment, for the first time, I could see how much he cared about her. As strange as whatever it was they had or did, he actually loved her.

I waited to see if he would give me that look that he always gave me. The look that said we still had some unfinished business. The look that said he wanted to take off all my clothes. But he never did. He only looked at me as though he wanted answers.

Answers that I couldn't give to him.

Kemp told me he would be around and he asked me if I could talk to West my way before he had to talk in his. Whatever the hell that meant.

I still hadn't told West about Sean and I having sex, so I added this Carla woman to the list as a topic of discussion.

Kemp drove away, and for the rest of the day, I couldn't seem to get him and Satin off of my mind.

Finally, later that evening, West and the kids came home.

"Sit down," I said to him.

West instantly looked tensed.

He took a seat beside of me after I kissed all the kids and sent them on their way.

"I wanted to tell you something before anyone else does." West waited for me to keep going. "When I was sixteen, I...I had sex with Sean, Drea's husband. Well, dead husband."

"What?" West looked confused.

"He was my first," I admitted.

West huffed. "So, you're telling me you slept with your sister's husband?"

"No. At the time, they weren't married. They'd just met."

"And that makes it better?"

"No, but it makes it different. I'm not proud of it. I don't even know how she found out about it, but she did. And I didn't want you to hear about it from anyone else."

West stood up.

"And I didn't want to have to hear something like this from you," he said in disappointment. "We've been going to counseling for months and not once did you mention something like this. She told us she could help us if we told her everything if we worked together. If we told each other all our secrets, and you left something like that out? What else are you keeping from me?" West asked.

"Nothing," I answered in a hurry, knowing I would never tell him I recently had sex with Kemp again.

"Nothing? Why don't I believe you?"

West headed towards the door.

"Wait, where are you going?"

"Anywhere, but here. Away from you," West answered just as he closed the door behind him. It seemed like he was always trying to get away from me and this house these days.

I exhaled loudly, realizing I hadn't got the chance to ask him about the woman named Carla.

I called West's phone a few times, but he never answered. A few minutes later Cheyenne, George's wife, texted me, stating she could hear West screaming in the living room from her bedroom. She asked me if everything okay.

I simply replied: No.

I knew he was probably venting to George about what I'd just told him, so I didn't call him again.

I just sat there.

Wondering if we should just give up.

If it wasn't one thing, it was another. And I was hoping this West and Carla thing was one big misunderstanding. It better be. West had better not be sleeping with her or worse.

Satin was missing, and Kemp seemed to think West knew something about it.

I couldn't think of any reason why he would have anything to do with Satin's disappearance, but I was just as curious as Kemp was as to why the wife of the man Satin had been sleeping with had come to see West.

What's the connection?

I glanced at the window and then I headed towards the front door.

If I know Kemp...

I walked outside and looked around.

Yep. There he is.

Kemp was parked across the street from my house. He must've come back at some time or the other, and now he was just sitting there.

I should've known he wouldn't be too far.

Actually, I was surprised he hadn't followed West.

As I walked towards the car, he got out of it.

"He doesn't know anything about Satin," I said to him, though I wasn't sure if I was telling a lie.

Kemp ran his fingers through his hair and leaned up against his car.

"I'll never forgive myself if something happens to her," he said. He didn't seem like himself. He didn't seem like himself at all.

"I can find anybody, but I can't seem to find my own wife. There were no cameras close enough to see Satin's apartment. I told her we needed cameras, but she didn't want them. She'd said, 'We're in these little ass apartments. Really, what's the worst that could happen?' I bet she hadn't seen this shit coming."

Kemp shook his head.

I felt bad for him. I felt sorry for him. Even though I didn't want to. I'd told him to leave me alone. He wasn't supposed to be here.

"Everything is going to be okay, Kemp. I'm sure you'll find her." Against my better judgement, I reached out my hand for him to hold it.

For a moment, he hesitated.

And then he took my hand.

Lava what the hell are you doing?

~***~

"I've been calling you for days!"

"And I've been fucking my husband for days so…what's your point?" Thea laughed.

Ying had been home for a while, but I understood they had some catching up to do.

We were at Drea's wedding rehearsal.

Drea and I had only spoken briefly. Things were still very awkward between us, but she insisted on not hearing what I had to say about what I'd done with Sean.

Every time I tried to bring up the conversation, she dismissed me. But she did make it clear she still wanted me in her wedding.

So, I was there.

And I was her matron of honor.

I was so uncomfortable and all I wanted to do was talk to my sister and explain.

I'd concluded Sean had to have told her about us.

He must've told her before he died.

Or once he found out he had cancer.

I was angry because he hadn't thought about what telling our secret would do to me.

He was dead.

I was still alive.

And I was the only one that had to live with the consequences.

The music started, and we got into our places and rehearsed for Drea's wedding day.

I couldn't help but to watch her and Boris. They seemed comfortable with each other, but they didn't seem like they were in love; well, at least she didn't.

He seemed to be head over heels in love with her and he probably had been for a very long time. Drea seemed as though she liked him. Or maybe she only loved him because he loved her. If she even loved him at all.

Maybe she just wanted to be with someone because she didn't want to be alone.

West was a groomsman in the wedding, but he was barely making eye contact with me. We'd talked about renewing our vows not too long ago, but I was pretty sure he didn't want to now. He probably didn't want his vows at all.

He was home but most days it was as though he wasn't even there.

Our marriage was falling apart.

Once rehearsal was over and everyone started to mingle, I walked outside of the church alone.

Her big day was only two days away, and I could only hope what she was doing would make her happy. I could only hope once she was married to someone else she could find a way to forgive me because I could see in her eyes that, as of right now, she didn't.

I felt like crying.

Just a while ago, I felt as though I was on top of the world. I was getting my life back on track but now I felt like it all had come tumbling down again.

My sister hated me.

My husband probably hated me too.

It seemed like the only person who wanted to be bothered with me at the moment was…

I raised my head and looked across the street from the church for his car.

He was there.

As always, he was always right there…

~***~

KEMP

I could see Lava looking towards me.

I was there.

Where else would I be?

My face was all over the T.V....*again.*

Pops had been arrested and about a handful of other men in connection with our network or organization.

The only big one they didn't have was me.

Or Satin.

But surprisingly, her name hadn't been mentioned, nor had they been willing to pay for any information about her.

Maybe Dedrick was protecting her. Maybe he'd lied and told them she hadn't had anything to do with any of the things we'd done.

They were offering fifty thousand dollars for any information that would lead to my arrest. So, as of now, I was laying low. Real low.

And I'd been depending on Lava.

She was helping me hide.

She'd gotten a hotel room for me in her name, so I wouldn't have to show my face and she'd even been getting me food.

I couldn't say I was surprised she was helping me out. We shared this weird connection neither of us wanted to admit, but she understood I needed to find Satin. I could deal with whatever else came after that. I just couldn't end up in jail before I figured out what happened to her.

I ran my hand across my almost bald head. Not having my hair didn't feel right. Lava had cut it down low for me, hoping to make me a little less noticeable while going in and out of the hotel. I only went into the hotel late at night when I assumed most people were asleep, and I always took the stairs and the back-entrance doors to enter and leave. If I went there at all. Most nights, if I slept, it was in my car.

Lava usually kept me informed with what was being said about me on the news. She and I were talking a lot more these days, and I could tell that she was trying to keep my mind off of what was going on.

It wasn't working.

I didn't feel like I was being followed anymore.

Maybe it had all been in my head.

With Pops in custody, I didn't know what to expect. I'd never got around to telling him about Satin.

I'd paid Hamid, from the bar, to drive to Washington and go by Satin's apartment building. He told me undercover officers were watching the building like a hawk, and it was best that I stayed away.

They were most likely waiting to see if either me or Satin would show up.

But there was still no sign of her.

Satin had disappeared without a trace.

And with this reward out for my arrest, I couldn't move how I wanted to move. I couldn't look for her like I needed to. And I was trying to stay out of Washington because of my run-in with Dedrick. He knew I'd been in town. He knew I was looking for Satin. He was just waiting on me to resurface.

We had connections all over the place, but I didn't want to reach out to any of them. They could easily set me up or turn me, and I couldn't take that chance.

Except with Hamid.

I couldn't say Hamid was a friend, but he was loyal. After all, I'd saved his life. As well as his wife's and child's.

He'd been caught up in some bad business a few years ago. It was the same year we bought the bar to use at our disposal.

It was our first time coming to Virginia and our only assignment was to get the bar up and running to serve its purpose.

Being that we were going to be there for a few months, we stayed in the very house that Satin had stayed in not too long ago. One night, I arrived at the place we were calling home, but I hadn't gone inside.

I'd heard the screams, so I followed the sound.

I stopped in front of the house two houses down and peered into the slightly raised window that allowed me to hear her cries.

Immediately, I spotted the gun.

Hamid was begging the man holding the gun. He told him that he would get him his money, and he asked him to let his wife and child go. Hamid was wearing a suit, so I figured he was a shady ass businessman that had screwed over the wrong people.

But once the man turned the gun towards the child, I intervened.

No, it wasn't any of my business, but I made it mine. I took the gun that I had in my waist and shot him through the window.

The lady screamed, and Hamid looked towards the window, as the man tumbled onto the floor.

Then I knocked on the door, and Hamid timidly answered. I told him I would be sending a few guys to clean up the mess, and that he now owed me a favor.

I told him I needed him to work for me.

I asked him to turn in his suit and tie and to run the bar.

And without questions, he did just that.

Ever since then, I'd been able to count on him, and to date, we'd never had any issues. He did what I told him to do.

Not to mention, he was the only connection, other than the one in South America, I had that didn't have to go through Pops first. He didn't have any ties to Satin's father, whatsoever.

Pops was still one of my biggest concerns.

I was sure he would've used every resource, every connection he had by now to get out of this mess, but he hadn't made a move.

That worried the fuck out of me.

What is he doing in there?

What is he saying?

I gotta get out of here! I gotta go!

Come on, Satin, baby, where are you?

I watched Lava walk back into the church.

I'd been following West for the past few days.

When he wasn't home, in class, or at his shop, he was mostly still going to the bar. Sometimes he would stop by

George and his wife's new house or visit his boys at the firehouse. Some nights he even slept there.

Lava told me what was going on in their marriage.

She told me Drea finally revealed what she knew about Lava and her husband.

Of course, I already knew the whole truth.

But I pretended not to know anything at all.

Lava still didn't know everything.

Drea left out that she'd used Tokyo to get revenge on Lava for what she'd done.

Since Drea hadn't mentioned it, neither did I.

It wasn't my place to tell Lava.

Besides, I'd handled it.

Initially.

Still, Drea was back in town, she was getting married, and appeared to be trying to get over the past. Lava said she didn't even want to talk about the situation. She even said Drea told her that she just wanted to forget about it. *And* she kept Lava in her wedding.

But I did still have one question though.

Where in the hell is Tokyo?

I couldn't use my resources to keep tabs on her the way I wanted to. Since Lava had told me she saw her, I wondered what she was up to.

I should've known if Drea was here, so was she.

Speeding past the church, I decided to get on the highway and go to Washington instead of the hotel.

I knew it was risky, but I couldn't just sit around and do nothing.

Carla hadn't been back to West's shop, and it was killing me not knowing what she could possibly be up to.

I just have to be careful.

That's all.

I just had to be smart.

~***~

LAVA

"Where did you go?"

"Outside to get some fresh air."

West approached me as soon as I walked back through the sanctuary doors. Everyone was still chatting, but West was preparing to leave.

"Where are you going?"

"Out with the guys to the bar. Drea said we're done. I'll be home later."

"West..."

I touched his chest before he could walk past me.

His phone started to vibrate before I could say anything else. He glanced down at it, and instinctively, so did I.

The number wasn't saved but the location underneath the number said Washington, D.C.

Carla?

"Who is that?"

West looked at me.

"Nobody."

"Who is nobody?"

West shook his head. "Like I said, it's nobody." That was all he'd said before brushing past me and heading out the church doors.

So, Kemp was right?

West and Carla were up to something.

And I was going to find out just what it was!

~***~

TOKYO

I smiled at Japan as I touched his hand.

He looked at me with love and, though I loved him, in that moment, I looked at him with regret.

I was about to make a horrible decision.

I was about to do something stupid.

Something I couldn't take back.

I was about to ruin Drea's wedding.

She isn't just going to play me like this!

After all I'd done for her!

For months, Drea and I were like a couple…minus the sex. We did everything else together.

Lived together.

Raised Japan together.

We were playing it by ear and simply living from day to day with no real plan. Then one day Drea wanted something different.

She said maybe she'd been going through a mid-life crisis. Maybe she was just so blinded by anger that she wasn't thinking straight. She had some type of panic attack and said she couldn't believe all she'd done. She couldn't believe what we'd done to Lava. She couldn't believe she'd gotten Kemp to kill her husband. She couldn't believe that she'd left her family and what we were doing—together. She said that, honestly, she wasn't into women.

Hell, neither was I before her.

I thought we were in it together, but she made it clear she wanted out.

Drea said she missed her life. She missed her family, her job, and her friends. She told me she was glad Lava hadn't ended up in prison or dead because of her rage.

She'd had some kind of epiphany.

And then she told me she was leaving.

She told me she couldn't stay there with me and the baby anymore.

Drea told me she was going home and for me to forget what we'd done. That she never wanted to see me again.

Those were the words she'd said to me.

She used me.

She'd used me to get revenge on her sister, and now, she had no use for me.

She was the only person I had, other than the baby.

Our connection—our relationship couldn't be defined, but if nothing else, I thought she was my friend. I thought what we felt for each other was real. She knew I'd been going through a lot but, apparently, it had been all about her and what she wanted.

She was mad at her sister, so she used me to get back at her. She wanted Lava to suffer so she convinced me to help her.

And it was all for what?

Japan giggled at me, and I almost changed my mind.

I almost drove away and never looked back again, but hate wouldn't let me do it. Hate wouldn't let me leave.

I hated Drea.

She'd helped me lose everything I had.

I got a divorce. I gave up my job. My only friends. Everything!

And I'll be damned if she gets a new beginning!

There was no happily ever after for her that didn't include me!

I wondered what would happen to Japan after all this was said and done. If I was caught. I wondered who would get him. I wondered where he would end up.

I loved him.

He is my son.

Even if we didn't share the same blood.

But I had to do this.

I had to stop this wedding.

And that's exactly what I was going to do.

I'd seen Kemp's face plastered all over the T.V. so I figured I didn't have to worry about him or his threats about being back in town. Besides, he'd told me to stay away from Lava. And I was.

He didn't say a damn thing about staying away from Drea.

I pulled right in front of the church.

I was sure by now Drea was probably standing in a white gown at the front of the church, about to vow to love and honor a man I was positive she didn't even like.

She was just trying to forget.

She was trying to forget what she'd done.

She was trying to forget her husband.

And she was trying to forget me.

I glanced at Japan one last time before I turned on the AC and got out of the car. But not before getting the gun out my purse.

I left the driver's side door wide open. I know, it kind of defeated the purpose of having on the air, but I was trying to keep him as cool as possible while making it easy for me to get into the car and drive away.

It would only take me a minute.

It didn't take long to shoot someone.

I glanced around me.

No one was outside, but the parking lot was full.

I adjusted the blonde wig I was wearing, and I placed on my sunglasses.

Slowly, I walked up the church steps.

I was hoping I'd waited long enough and everyone was seated inside of the sanctuary, but I was prepared to knock out the hostess if I had to.

Luckily, no one was there.

The teal and yellow flower arrangements made me cringe. Drea loved the color yellow.

As I inched towards the double doors, my heart was racing but I wasn't nervous.

More than anything else, I was upset.

Ever since I was a little girl, life for me had never been easy. My father ran out on my mother with my eighteen-year-old babysitter when I was ten. I never saw him again.

Ever.

After that, my mother was never quite the same. She took care of me, but that was about it. She bought me anything I asked for, but she never had time for me. She never paid any attention to me. And once her parents, my grandparents, died in a boating accident when I was sixteen, she completely lost her marbles.

I was an only child, and so was she, but I tried to be there for her. She just didn't let me.

My mother started to drink herself half to death, and I started to act out. I'd wanted to get as far away from her as possible one day, so I worked hard in school to get a scholarship but at home I gave her pure hell.

I didn't listen to her.

I didn't respect her.

For the most part, most days, she pretended as though I wasn't even there. And after a while, I just got used to feeling like I was all alone.

Until I started to date West.

He was a little older than I was and I think he liked that I was a little rough around the edges. He knew I was damaged, but it seemed to turn him on.

Did I love him?

Back then, as much as I could.

Though his family thought I was bad for him, in a way, I think he saved me. He came into my life just as I was starting to feel like giving up, and he kept me focused.

And then he had the crazy idea of getting married.

It was his idea.

Not mine.

Though I knew marrying him wasn't exactly what I'd wanted to do, I did it because he was the only thing I was sure of at the time.

He was the only person that loved me.

Then he changed his mind.

I was used to feeling unwanted, so I agreed to get the marriage annulled. Then I accepted the scholarship to a college I was going to turn down just to be with him.

The marriage was already over when I found out that I was pregnant. I hadn't bothered to tell West or anyone else. I stole the money from my mama for the abortion. I woke up later that night, in pain and bleeding all over the place. The saddest part of all was my poor excuse of a mother was too drunk to drive me to the hospital.

I had to call the ambulance.

I'd lost so much blood.

At the hospital that night, I found something with the abortion had gone wrong and there was a good chance I would never have kids again.

My mother didn't even bother to show up at the hospital. And I didn't call West. For three days, I just laid there in pain, going through it all on my own.

A week later I was gone.

The scholarship was the best thing that ever happened to me. I was free. I thought maybe life away from my mother and away from Virginia would be better.

I would have a fresh start.

But I guess a better life just wasn't in the cards for me.

I had to find a part-time job for extra money.

I hopped in and out of bed with anyone who showed me just the slightest bit of attention or interest.

And then, two weeks before graduating from college, my mother died. She got sick with pneumonia, went to the hospital, and never came back home.

Her best friend, who was just as bad off as my mother had been, called me and told me the news.

We didn't have any close family, so I told her that there was no need for a funeral. I told her to have her cremated and do what she wanted to do with the ashes.

I didn't want them.

I hadn't even seen or even spoken to my mother in almost four years. For me, for years, she was already dead.

After college, I found a job within three months and eventually, I met Jerell.

In the beginning, he was just like any other man.

Sweet. Charming. The whole nine yards.

I was surprised to find he was also from Virginia, just a city over from where I'd grown up.

I did everything he asked of me.

And then he asked me to marry him.

For a few years, we were happy. At least, I was. He was good to me and I thought I was finally in a happy place. Then came the affairs, and they never seemed to stop. There was always someone else. Some other woman I was sharing my husband with.

I started threatening to leave him and he asked if we could have a fresh start. He asked me to move back to Virginia with him, closer to his family, and he told me that he would never cheat again.

He lied.

Hell, it might've even got worse once we came back *home*.

Why didn't I leave him sooner?

At first, I wondered…for what?

Where would I go?

I'd found a job already, but I would be in Virginia all alone, so I stayed with him. I put up with it. Started going to the meetings and that's when I met Drea.

It'd been nothing but even more chaos ever since.

She made an already fucked up life even worse. At least before her I had a job, a piece of a marriage, and some kind of friends. Even though I was sure I would've had to tell Lava the truth about West and I eventually. But no, I thought Drea was my friend. I thought she was more than a friend.

But Drea was the devil.

I pulled on the handle of one of the double doors.

Slowly, I peeked inside.

Drea was standing at the front of the church holding Boris's hands.

I knew who he was.

She used to call him a snake back in the day when we would chat at the bar over drinks.

She couldn't stand him, though she knew he had a thing for her. And now all of a sudden, she comes back home and months later they're getting married.

No one seemed to notice me peeking into the church.

I could hear the pastor as he told Boris to repeat after him.

I looked down at the gun in my right hand then I looked back at the door that led out the church.

The shock of what I was about to do would surely give me a minute or two to get outside and drive away before anyone came looking for me.

I knew once I pulled the trigger I wouldn't be able to take it back, and I didn't want to.

I was tired of people treating me any kind of way.

I was tired of people treating me like shit!

She should've just let me be!

Hearing Drea start to speak caused me to look through the crack in the door again.

She was reciting her vows and my blood started to boil.

My hand that was holding the gun started to shake, as I slowly slid my foot in front of the door to hold it open.

The safety was already off.

I knew it was now or never.

"Drea, do you take Boris Noah Davis, to be your…"

Now!

Hurriedly, I stuck my arm in the door, aiming right for Drea and fired twice.

Boom!

Boom!

Without lingering, I ran immediately after yells filled the church.

I was out the church, into my car, and pulling off in less than twenty seconds. Still holding the gun in one hand and the steering wheel with the other, I pressed on the gas, speeding down the street. I didn't even breathe until I was at least three minutes down the road.

"Oh, my God!" Finally, I inhaled then exhaled and screamed at the top of my lungs. And then I started to laugh.

I hope I got her!

I hope she's dead!

"Calm down, Tokyo. Calm down," I spoke to myself.

"Don't worry Japan. Mommy's fine…"

I looked behind me.

What?

What!

I slammed on my brakes and a bus almost slammed into me from behind.

My heart dropped into the pit of my belly as I got out of the car and rushed around to the back door on the passenger's side.

No!

The baby…my son…Japan…wasn't in his car seat or anywhere in the back seat.

My baby was gone!

****

Chapter SEVEN

LAVA

Everyone was running around and screaming.

The entire church was in complete chaos, but I just stood there.

Frozen.

Nothing but my eyes were able to move.

Drea was on the floor.

Surrounded by anyone who could get to her.

I saw red.

On her dress, I saw red.

Then the sight of her dress disappeared and I saw West.

He was coming towards me.

"Lava? Lava? Baby? Look at me."

I am looking at you.

And then my eyes started to look for the kids.

One. Two.

Where's Three?

Oh, okay, Three.

Four.

Five.

They were all okay.

"Lava? Lava?"

West started to shake me.

Ouch.

Ouch!

What is that?

Pain. Something didn't feel right.

"Oh, no! Lava!"

West yelled, but I couldn't understand what he was saying anymore.

Throbbing pain hit me like a tidal wave.

"Lava! Baby! You've been shot! You've been shot!"

What?

~***~

"How is she?"

Mama smiled at me. "Both of you are going to be okay."

I'd been standing right behind Drea, holding her bouquet of flowers as she was about to say her wedding vows.

Next thing I know, we heard gun shots and all hell broke loose.

Everything was so crazy. I didn't notice that I'd been shot. I'd been shot in my right arm, and Drea had been shot in the back, near her right shoulder.

"I still can't believe someone would come into a church and…"

Mama stopped talking.

"Do they know who it was?"

"No. A church of one hundred plus folks, and no one saw a thing. No one noticed anyone with a gun. No one saw anything unusual, other than the double door closing once the shots were fired. But no one saw who it was."

I didn't know what to think.

Drea and I had been shot, but who were the shots intended for?

Me?

Her?

Boris?

We couldn't be sure.

West came into the room, and mama kissed my forehead and told me she would be back soon.

"How are you feeling?"

"I'm okay. It's just an arm, I'm going to live."

West smiled.

"Aw, man," he joked, as though he was disappointed.

"Mama says they don't know who did it."

"They don't, but I'm hoping that they find out soon. What the fuck were they thinking shooting into a crowded church? My kids were in there! And they shot my wife!"

West was upset, and he had every right to be.

"Where are the kids?"

"They're at Janay's."

West sat beside my bed. "They're only going to keep you for a day. I'm not sure about Drea. And the police want to speak to you, eventually."

"Okay."

West looked at me confused. "You seem a little too calm about all of this. Do you know someone that would want to shoot you? Or Drea?"

I shook my head. "No. Maybe it was your new little girlfriend Carla," I said to him, intentionally bringing her up to discuss her.

Sure.

I could've gotten shot anywhere else, but I hadn't. I was still here. And for now, I didn't know what to feel.

"Carla? How do you know about Carla? Carla is…"

"Knock, knock."

Thea walked in with food.

"Girl, don't be trying to check out on me!"

West stood up and allowed Thea to take his seat.

"I'll be back in a little bit," West said, kissing my forehead then he was gone.

"Nothing like a little shooting to bring a marriage back together," Thea laughed.

"Shut up. You'll say anything, won't you?"

"You damn right. This my mouth. Who gonna stop me? Anyway, what did you do?"

"I didn't do anything, to anybody. But…"

"What?"

I shook my head. "It wouldn't be Tokyo, right?"

"Tokyo? Why would she shoot up Drea's wedding?"

I shrugged. "I mean, she was just standing outside of her bachelorette party that night. Remember? And you saw them arguing at the store that day."

"Yeah, but they were arguing over you. I doubt that was serious enough to make her shoot at her during her wedding."

"Maybe not." I tried to think. "Then who?"

Thea shrugged. "Maybe it's something to do with Drea or Boris that none of us would know about. Maybe a crazy, jealous ex or something. Whatever it is, it has to be pretty serious for them to just start firing into a church on somebody's wedding day. It took one cold, heartless, you know what to do something like that. Hell, that is right up Tokyo's alley, isn't it? Cold and heartless."

Thea reached for the remote to the room's T.V.

I was in deep thought.

And then I realized something.

I didn't have to think too much because I was sure that Kemp had been somewhere watching the church all along.

I was sure he saw the shooter.

He was never too far away.

But if he saw them, then the questions were:

Why hadn't he stopped them?

Why had he let them get away?

~***~

KEMP

I watched Dedrick as he loaded the back of his truck.

His wife just stood there on the front porch with her arms folded.

He kept stopping to answer his phone but once he was done loading the truck he stood in front of her.

This is what divorce looks like?

Everyone Satin and I personally knew or that was close enough for us to truly care about had been married for years. We didn't believe in divorce. Most of the time issues could be worked through, and that was part of the reason why I'd encouraged Lava to try things with her husband again. No matter what I felt for her and no matter what either of them did.

I'd been away from Virginia and back in Washington for three days, still trying to find something that could lead me to Satin.

Still nothing yet.

Finally, Dedrick got into the truck and I contemplated whether to follow him or to stay behind and see where his wife would go or what she would do once he was gone.

I'd been alternating watching them almost all day. A part of me was glad that I'd gotten out of VA because a few government officials had been in town lately.

Hamid had been questioned.

They'd went by the bar, and they wanted to know the last time I'd been there. They wanted to know if he knew anything about Pop's organization, but he didn't. He didn't know much, other than I was involved in some pretty deep shit, but he never bothered to ask questions.

Once I knew he was loyal, I drew up some fake paperwork as though he'd purchased the bar from me. As far as anyone could tell, he was the owner of the bar, which was probably the only reason it was still open.

Because of that move.

He told me they asked about Satin and I, but he told them he hadn't seen either of us in a while.

I was still on the T.V. with the headline of being wanted in connection to multiple murders. Other than that, not much else about what was going on was being shown.

I didn't know if they still had Pops in custody or if he was being held in the U.S. or in Cairo. I didn't know every detail about what they knew or if they'd made more arrests.

I didn't know much of anything.

All I knew was now, even after I found Satin, it was going to be harder for us to disappear.

I decided to follow Dedrick.

He hadn't moved far from his wife.

And the other day I discovered he'd resigned from his so-called position with Homeland Security.

I was assuming he would no longer be undercover. And if his wife was a part of that cover, that was probably part of the reason he was letting go.

Maybe he never really loved her at all.

I wasn't sure why he thought Satin wouldn't warn me about who he really was. Maybe he actually wanted Satin for himself. Maybe he thought they actually had something special. Satin did have that effect on men.

She always made them fall for her, only to find out they'd been played by her or she'd disappeared without an explanation. Or without a goodbye. And that's what happened to the lucky ones. Two of them weren't that lucky. They were dead.

Either way, I still found it interesting he told her the truth. He'd been lying about who he was for years to everyone else, yet, he'd come clean to her.

If nothing else, I found it odd.

Dedrick started to unload his truck just as a black car pulled into the driveway and parked behind him.

He walked up to the car and started to talk and then…

I pressed on the gas just as Dedrick started to run in my direction.

The black car swerved out the driveway and sped behind me.

That motherfucker knew I was watching him!

The car turned on its sirens as I ran a red light.

Cars swerved around me, as I tried to form a plan.

We had a safe house that wasn't too far away, but I wasn't sure how safe it was anymore. I'd been avoiding it since Pops had been arrested.

I couldn't be sure how much Dedrick and his crew knew. I couldn't be sure how much Pops had told them by now, but I didn't have a choice.

I had to get off the streets.

And I was sure they'd called for backup.

I turned onto Whitehead Street, knowing the house was less than a mile away. I tried to lose the car and, after hearing other sirens in the distance, I knew it was now or never.

I had to get out.

I caught sight of a bus and I sped in front of it. The bus slammed on its brakes just as I'd hoped it would and I turned onto a side street, parking behind a random house.

Sirens seemed to be coming from every direction, so I got out the car and started to run.

On foot, I moved from backyard to backyard and jumped over a few fences. I ran hard, fast, constantly looking behind me. After a while, the wails of the sirens, started to get further and further away.

I'd lost them.

Still, I kept moving. By the time the safe house was in sight, the sirens could no longer be heard.

Pops had little random properties in different cities all over the world just in case we were ever in a jam. He even had some properties that were being rented as an additional stream of revenue. Usually, we didn't stop at one of the houses unless we absolutely had to. In this situation, I didn't feel as though I had a choice.

They would be looking for me.

Waiting for me.

So, I had to hide.

Approaching the door, I ran my hand across the top of the doorframe until it hit the key.

I grabbed it and hurried inside.

Locking the door behind me, I found the light switch.

"Ah, I was wondering when you were going to show up," I heard a voice say from behind me.

Slowly, I turned around…

~***~

LAVA

"Chile, I guess when God says NOT NOW and NOT SO," I joked.

Drea caught on to it and smiled. "Right. I guess he really didn't want me to marry Boris, huh? Did I really have to get shot though?"

I was preparing to leave the hospital and decided to go by and see Drea. Drea's blood pressure was still sky high, so they weren't sure when she would be released.

"I talked to the police, but no one saw who did it."

"I know who did it," Drea said.

"What? Who? Were they trying to shoot you?"

"Yes, *she* was."

"She?"

Drea looked at me. I couldn't quite read her face. She'd said *she*.

Hmmm. I thought about something.

Thea and I were right. This had her name written all over it.

"Tokyo?"

Drea rolled her eyes.

"She did this, didn't she? Why? Why would she want to ruin your wedding? Why would she want to shoot you? She was outside of Janay's house the night of your bachelorette party. And the two of you were arguing at the store. Why? What's the real reason? What's going on, Drea?"

"You know, when I first found out about you and Sean, a long time ago, I was devastated. I couldn't believe my little sister had been one of my husband's whores."

"Drea, it wasn't like that. I was only sixteen. You weren't married to Sean, and I didn't think you ever would be."

"So that makes it okay?"

"No, it doesn't. I'm sorry. I don't know what I was thinking. But he wasn't your husband at the time. It never happened while he was your husband."

Drea rolled her eyes at me.

"You're my sister! Some things, you just don't do."

I felt bad, I truly did. But what I wanted to know about was Tokyo. What about Tokyo?

"There were so many women. Yet, somehow, I managed to keep loving him. But when I found out he'd had you...that changed something inside of me," Drea admitted. "Your sins always catch up with you. Yours did. And I guess me almost dying on my wedding day was mine attempting to catch up with me."

"What are you talking about, Drea?"

"Tokyo shot me. And you. But she was trying to shoot me. Just me."

"Why?"

"Why else?" Drea asked sarcastically. "Because she loves me, duh."

What?

"It was me."

West peeked his head into the room and I waved him away.

"I put Tokyo up to sleeping with West and ruining your marriage. Everything she did was for me."

Drea looked me right in the eyes, as my mouth fell open.

I'd heard what she said, but I couldn't process it. I couldn't understand it. I couldn't accept it.

"I was so angry when I found out the truth. I hated you. I hated Sean. I was in a bad place. Sean's trifling ass had been cheating on me for years, and I'd been dealing with it all on my own. I was too embarrassed to tell anyone what I was going through. I was too ashamed. I had it all. Everyone thought I was strong and successful, but I couldn't make my husband keep his dick in his pants, and I was afraid to admit it. To Mama. To my sisters. And then Sean was diagnosed with cancer. I guess he wanted to come clean before he died so one day he told me. He told me he'd had sex with you a few times. And that was the last straw. That was my breaking point."

My arm started to ache as I backed away from her. Drea sat up, and surprisingly, she had a smirk on her face.

"I wanted to hurt you. And I did. Tokyo and I met at these little meetings we used to go to. One night, I was talking about you. Not only did I find out the two of you worked together, but she also admitted she'd been married to West. She knew you didn't know about their past relationship. And she was on the fence with telling you because she wanted to be your friend.

"Tokyo and I had become close...in a different kind of way. And then we had this...this night together. We explored each other in a way that I'd never experienced before. That night meant more to her than it had to me. I could tell she'd started to feel something for me that I wasn't sure I felt, but I knew I could use it to my benefit. We both had gone through so much for love. And it was trifling ass women—like you—that were constantly getting in our way!"

"You mean to tell me..."

I couldn't finish my sentence.

"Sean was already dying. But you? You had it all. The house full of kids. The faithful husband. It wasn't fair. Not with your dirty, little secret. Not with what you'd done to me. So, I wanted to see just how faithful he was. I wasn't you. I would've never came on to him. But from what Tokyo told me, things ended a little abruptly between the two of them. It's nothing like unfinished business to spark up an old flame. So, I talked her into coming on to West just to see what he would do. Just to mess up your marriage, too."

Rage started to consume me, and I became as hot as hell's fire!

My own sister…

"At first, she was just going to sleep with him, make him fall in love with her, then expose him and ruin your marriage. But things got interesting. You started to trust her. You told her about the fire at the mayor's house. And then when you thought you killed Satin… It became somewhat fun for me to watch your life crumbling all around you. It felt like…justice. Until it didn't. Everything got crazy. Satin ended up being alive. And you just wouldn't let West go. You wanted your husband, through it all. You just wouldn't give up. And then the fun finally came to an end. I thought causing so much havoc was what I wanted. In the end, I realized I was just hurt and I'd gone entirely too far. So, I ran away with Tokyo. I wasn't sure why, but I just knew at the time I didn't want to be here. Hell, I couldn't be here after Kemp threatened me to stay away from you."

"Wait… What did you say? Did you say Kemp?"

"Yes. He was going to kill Tokyo for all she'd done to you, but I was there so he spared her life. He told us both to stay the hell away from you or he would kill us. I believed him. After all, he did finish off Sean for me."

"Kemp killed Sean?"

"Yep. He was taking too long to die, and I just wanted him dead already. I just wanted to be free. So, Kemp finished him off. In return, he said I was never to go near you again."

Kemp hadn't mention any of this to me!

Ughhh!

"So, he knew it was you? He knew about you and Tokyo? He knew you'd been the brains behind Tokyo's actions? He knew you were the cause of everything I went through?"

"Stop sounding like the fucking victim! You were the cause of everything you went through!" Drea growled.

Why hadn't Kemp told me?

He should've told me about Drea!

"Anyway, I left with Tokyo. For a few months, I was with her and the baby."

"Baby?"

"Yep. Kemp gave her the baby that George and Satin had together. That was her 'stay the hell away from Lava' *present*, more or less."

What!

That's what he did with the baby? He gave it to Tokyo? He gave the baby to my enemy?

I had a headache.

"We drove all the way to Louisiana. Found someone to rent us an apartment since we both had plenty of savings. If nothing else, we were friends, but I knew Tokyo felt something more. I'd used her desperate need for love and have someone in her corner to get her to do what I wanted her to do. And maybe…maybe I did see her as a friend but once the high of what I'd done to you started to wear off and once I started to sit around and *think*… I realized I'd made a terrible mistake. I couldn't give her what she wanted from me. I didn't want to be with a woman. And I missed home. I missed my job. I missed Mama. You? Um, not so much. But I realized staying with Tokyo and leaving behind my entire life wasn't what I really wanted to do. So, one day I left."

West started to knock at the door, and I screamed at him. He stopped knocking.

"She called me like crazy. Crying. Begging. Screaming. I felt bad. At the time, all I could see was getting back at you. I didn't see what it could do to her. She'd had a horrible childhood. A horrible marriage. And I'd been a horrible friend." Drea decided to lie back down.

"Eventually, I stopped answering her calls. She called me all day, every day, so I changed my number. And then she showed up. I told her I was sorry, but I'd moved on. I told her I was dating Boris. I convinced him I'd always felt something for him, and since we'd known each other for years, I told him we should take a chance and just get married. He's always wanted me, so he agreed and found me a position at the firm he was going to be working for in Atlanta. I thought I wanted to be back here. But being here just makes me sad. It reminds me of everything that happened. Everything my husband did to me. Of what you did to me. And what I did to you."

I just stood there with tears of anger flowing from my eyes. I know what I did was wrong, but all she'd done to me was just pure evil! All she had to do was come to me. Hell, we could've talked it out, even fought it out like normal sisters do. But no, she had to go to the extreme. She'd done the unthinkable. She'd done...the unforgivable.

"I messed up. I did. I should've never had sex with Sean. But what you did to me..."

"Hurt? Good. Then it was a job well done." Drea stood firm on her thoughts that I'd started this. That I'd caused and deserved what she'd done to me.

Maybe I had.

"At the store, Tokyo and I were arguing. She didn't want me to get married to Boris. She told me I was all that she had, other than the baby, and that she felt like I'd used her. I did, though I didn't admit that to her. I just told her I'd been confused and I just wanted her to leave me alone. Guess she said fuck that, huh?"

I was so conflicted by it all. I didn't know what to do with what I was feeling. One side of me wanted to beat the shit out of Drea. The other side of me wanted to hug her, knowing that after finding out the truth on both ends, we would probably never be able to mend what was broken. Our relationship from this day forward would never be the same.

"If I could change what I'd done, for Tokyo's sake, I would. And I would've confronted you for sleeping with Sean. I know that's what I should've done. But at the time, I wanted more. I was broken mentally, emotionally, and all I wanted was revenge. I don't care if you ever forgive me because I don't think I'll ever forgive you. But we can call it even. I just thought you should know the truth. In the end, that's what everyone wants. They just want the truth. And now you have it."

Drea half-smiled at me then she turned her back to me. As though she hadn't just blown up my world. As though she didn't even care about the pain I was feeling inside.

For a while, I just stood there. Stuck on what to do or say next. I wasn't sure we would ever get past this.

How could we?

And Kemp?

How could he not tell me the truth? How could he not tell me what he knew about Drea and Tokyo?

Finally, I forced myself to walk towards the door.

I looked back at her, one last time before shutting the room door behind me.

"You okay?" West asked as soon as he saw me.

I shook my head. "No. And I'm not sure I ever will be," was all I said.

~***~

KEMP

"Where is she?"

Dedrick had been holding me at gun point for a while.

I knew I could take the gun from him if I wanted to but since he didn't seem to be trying to take me to jail I wanted to know if he knew anything that was useful. Anything that might help me figure out if his wife…well ex-wife, had anything to do with Satin's disappearance.

"What did you do to her?"

"I didn't do anything to her. I'm looking for her."

"Where would she go?"

"You tell me," I said.

Dedrick stared at me. "If I hadn't gone by her apartment, I would've thought you were trying to play me. But her apartment had all the signs of a struggle. All the signs of a kidnapping. Who would want to take her?"

"I don't know."

"And she wouldn't have just left?"

"If she was going to do that, she wouldn't have told me anything about you or what you told her, now would she?"

I was going back and forth with myself on whether I wanted to kill him once I took the gun from him. Or if I wanted to wait.

"You're going to jail. You know that, don't you? But not until you tell me how to find Satin."

"I told you. I don't know. Shit, I'm looking for her too." I stared at him. "You fell for her, didn't you?"

Dedrick didn't answer.

He didn't have to. I already knew.

"Where would she be?"

"She would be with me if someone hadn't taken her."

"Who?"

"If I knew who took her, they would be dead," I grilled him.

"And you were following me, for what? You think I know where she is? You think I have her?"

"Or your wife."

"Carla?" Dedrick questioned.

"Yes, Carla."

"Why would you think she would know where Satin is?"

Dedrick glared at me. Suddenly, his phone started to ring, and he took his eyes off me for only a second to see who it was.

And that's when I made my move.

I lunged at him. I caught him by surprise. Before he had a chance to react, I already had his gun in my hand.

Dedrick tried to come at me, but I shot him in the leg.

He growled in pain as I snatched his phone out his hand and stomped on it. I watched him fall to the floor.

"Who does Carla know in Fairfax, Virginia?"

Dedrick didn't answer me.

I pulled the trigger, aiming for the side of his head but missing on purpose.

"Who does she know in Fairfax?"

Dedrick glared at me. "I don't know."

I wondered if he was telling the truth.

"Would she have something done to Satin?"

"No." Derick huffed.

"How can you be sure?"

"I guess we can never really be sure of anything, can we?" Dedrick replied just as I was about to squeeze the trigger. But another question came to mind.

"Where's Pops? Satin's father? Is he here? In Washington?"

The pain that had been on Dedrick's face was replaced by disappointment. "We had him. He was right there. In our custody. We had him. But I guess he got to one of us."

Dedrick took off his tie and tied it above the wound in his leg. He shrieked in agony, and then he eyed me with hatred. "He was being watched around the clock. We left for the night and came back to find the two men guarding him dead and Satin's father gone. Apparently, no one saw anything. No one knew how he got away. All the security footage from that night is missing. We still don't know who was behind helping him escape. He's gone. And I have a feeling we won't ever find him again."

Shit.

I wasn't surprised. But now I knew I would be hearing from him soon.

"You're the next best thing. You're our only shot at getting close to him again. You're his right-hand man." Dedrick panted in pain.

Pops was out, and he was going to be pissed! The same man that should've been dead already was the same man that had been involved in his arrest.

The smart thing to do was to go ahead and take care of Dedrick, but it wasn't the best thing to do.

Not with Satin still missing.

He cared about her, so I needed him alive. I needed his help. I needed his resources on the inside.

I shot him in his other leg.

"You motherfu—" Dedrick howled.

"The only reason I didn't put one in your goddamn head is because you obviously care about finding Satin just as much as I do. Your ex-wife knows something. Find out what it is. Find Satin. I'll kill you next time. You have my word."

I left Dedrick bleeding out, shot in both legs, to figure out how he was going to get help. I found his truck parked a few houses down. Had I been paying attention, I would've spotted it before going inside.

His truck was still loaded with his shit in the back of it, and it looked like everything was still there. The door was unlocked and after fucking with the wires I finally got it to start then drove away. I passed the house just in time to see that Dedrick had made his way to the door and was sliding onto the porch.

He was going to make it. He was going to find out what Carla knew. And he was going to help me find Satin.

And then he would be coming for me.

And when he does...I would be ready.

~***~

LAVA

West and I walked inside of Cheyenne and George's new home.

It was beautiful.

"How are you feeling?"

"I've been better."

West touched the small of my back.

The talk we'd had the day after leaving the hospital was everything.

I'd cried like never before while telling him what Drea told me. I told him everything. I told him every detail about having sex with Sean. Why I did it and why I never said anything about it. I told him what Drea had told me about what she'd done and why. And about Tokyo. I even told him what it was about Kemp that intrigued me.

And then, for the first time, West really broke down why he'd cheated on me. It wasn't out of boredom or some unfinished business or love he had for Tokyo. It wasn't because he was tired of me or because I wasn't giving him enough sex. It was simply because he thought he could get away with it.

His words, not mine.

He said that's all it was in the beginning.

They had a moment, she kissed him, and he didn't stop her. When there weren't any repercussions after they had sex the first time, he simply kept doing it because he wanted to. Over time, he fell in love with her all over again.

He'd said he would never understand why I didn't leave him. He'd never understand why I loved him so much. But he was glad I'd stayed. Glad I wanted to give us another chance. He said now it was his turn to stay and forgive me.

Carla was investigating something that involved one of the men that worked for West. She'd actually come to his shop that day to visit West's employee, Marvin, but he wasn't there. After speaking with West for a while, they exchanged contact information, and she told him to have Marvin reach out to her the next day. It was confidential, so West didn't even know what it was about.

However, Marvin never came back to work, which he'd never told me. He'd said we hadn't been talking much so he'd never gotten around to mentioning it. Since then, he and Carla had been playing phone tag. She'd called his shop and left a message. He'd called her back to tell her he hadn't seen or heard from Marvin, but she hadn't answered her phone. Then that night at the church, she was returning his call again. She'd left a voicemail.

That was it.

He'd meant it when she said she was nobody.

To him, she wasn't.

He swore to me it was nothing more to the situation, and that they didn't know each other. He continued to assure me that her visit had nothing to do with him.

So whatever Kemp thought about Carla and West was wrong.

At least, where West was concerned.

If Carla did have anything to do with Satin's disappearance or knew something about it, West sure as hell wasn't involved.

I hadn't seen or heard from Kemp, but I was still mad at him. I was mad because he could've told me the truth. He could've told me what he'd done. I didn't understand how he could pretend to care about me but not tell me what my own sister had done to me.

In some twisted way, maybe he thought not telling me was best. Maybe he thought he'd handled the situation.

But I'd deserved to know.

And I hated him.

I hated Tokyo.

But I hated Drea even more.

I'd talked to Mama.

She was so heartbroken by everything that had gone on between us. She was constantly trying to get Drea and I together, but neither of us would agree to it. Declora and Janay seemed to have squashed their little problem, considering that the one between Drea and I was much bigger.

I hadn't spoken to Drea and I wasn't sure if I ever would. After all, what was left to say?

According to Drea, Tokyo had been responsible for shooting us, but no one had seen her.

But when I saw Cheyenne come back into the room with a baby in her arms, something told me we all would be seeing Tokyo a lot sooner rather than later.

"How did you get the baby?" I asked Cheyenne.

"Excuse me? I was about to introduce you. We—"

"He's George's baby. By Satin." The baby was a spitting image of George, just with Satin's complexion and her beautiful dark hair. Immediately, I knew he was the baby Kemp had given to Tokyo.

"How did you get him? He was with Tokyo. How did you get him?"

George stood there.

There was no way that either of them could deny it.

"How did you get him from Tokyo?"

"He's mine," George spoke up. "He should've been with me from the very beginning. Not Tokyo."

Cheyenne held him close to her.

West looked confused.

"We were running late to your sister's wedding," Cheyenne finally said. "We heard a baby whining from a car, so we went to take a look. George opened the car door, and as soon as he saw him, he started to freak out. He started saying he was his son."

Cheyenne passed him to George.

"Of course, I had no idea what he was talking about. I had no idea he was supposed to even have a child out there, but I couldn't deny the resemblance. No one can. He looks just like him."

The baby cooed.

I had a bad feeling.

Tokyo had a few screws loose and if she found out that they had the baby…

"It was my idea to take him. We've always wanted a baby so badly. We were talking about adoption. And since George was sure the baby was his, with no one around, we took him, ran to our car, and drove away. George's brother is a doctor, as you know, so we went straight to his house and he told us he would run a DNA test. He's in fact George's son. And we're not giving him back."

West asked a few questions and then George spoke to me. "Why are you saying Tokyo had the baby? Where is Satin?"

"I don't know. But Drea told me Tokyo has been raising him all of this time."

"Drea?"

"Long story," West answered.

George handed the baby back to Cheyenne.

"Well I don't care who had him. He's with his father now, and he isn't going anywhere. If anybody thinks they are going to take him from me, they'll have to kill me first."

I touched the stitched hole in my arm as West followed George down to his basement.

George had better be careful with what he wished for, and even more careful with his words.

Tokyo had a hell of a way of coming after anything she thought was hers.

****

CHAPTER EIGHT

KEMP

"Kemp?"

"Lava."

I'd called her private.

"The FBI and everyone else in the entire world seems to be looking for you. They came to my house. They wanted to know about our past relationship. Obviously, they've done some digging and I came up. They wanted to know the last time I saw you. They said you shot someone, and they won't stop looking for you." Lava took a deep breath.

"And you lied to me."

"What?"

"You knew about Drea and Tokyo the whole time—"

"Not the whole time," I interrupted her. "And I took care of it."

"You took care of it?" she huffed. "I guess that's why Tokyo shot me then, huh?"

"What the fuck are you talking about?"

I knew I should've killed her that day at the hotel.

"She was trying to shoot Drea, but she ended up shooting both of us."

"Are you okay?"

"Yes. No thanks to you. You should've told me. How could you not tell me about *my* sister? My own sister tried to ruin my life, mess up my marriage, and even put me in jail. And you knew that. But instead of telling me, you killed her husband for her and just told her to go away."

"I thought I was doing the right thing for you at the time, Lava. I handled it. I could've killed your sister and Tokyo that day, but I didn't want to hurt you. She would've died, and you would've never known the truth. I didn't want to put you through any more than you'd been through already."

"You should've killed them. You should've killed both of them. But you handled it, as you said."

She was angry at the wrong person.

"Look, yeah, they told me the truth. They were supposed to disappear and never bother you again. All I cared about was you and helping you get your life back on track."

Lava was silent.

"But I was helping you. When your life was blowing up, I was helping you hide, and bringing you food. You were confiding in me and I was confiding in you. It never crossed your mind to just tell me what you knew about Drea? About Tokyo?"

"No."

Lava was silent. "Just go, Kemp. Just…go," she said finally.

"I can't leave without Satin."

"But you don't know where she is. Maybe she left without you. Have you even considered that?"

"She wouldn't."

"How do you know?"

"Because I know her." I waited on her to say something else, but she didn't. "I was calling to see if West and Carla—"

"West and Carla have nothing to do with Satin's disappearance. Well, at least West doesn't. Carla came to West's auto shop that day about a legal matter of one of his employees. That's it. No secret affair, no plan or plotting, no working together to hide Satin—nothing. I even listened to the voicemail she left him."

Damn.

"If Carla knows where Satin is, West isn't a part of that mess," Lava concluded.

I'd been lying low for a little over a week, relying on Hamid to make every single one of my moves. I'd tried to go back to my car after ditching Dedrick's truck, but it was surrounded by the FBI. I talked Hamid into coming to Washington to help me out. He put a rental car and a hotel room in his name for me and handled a few other things. In return, I transferred him a monetary incentive.

I was paranoid.

Dedrick had me on the news what seemed like twenty-four-seven. He was clearly pissed about being shot in both of his legs, but he'd lived. And he could still use them, so it was all good.

In his interview, he'd said I was dangerous and a threat to society. He also mentioned he was looking for my wife. He never said her name, so I knew he'd said the comment just for me. Just in case I was watching. Just in case I was listening.

"Lava…"

"George has his son. Tokyo left him in a car at the church while she… Anyway, George and his wife saw him and took him. I'm sure Tokyo is going crazy looking for him."

"Oh well. That's on her. She should've stayed away like I told her to."

Lava took a deep breath. "Kemp, I don't ever want to see you or hear from you again. I just want you to leave me alone. For good. Forever. Just don't come back here anymore." Without hesitating, she hung up.

I could tell she was still upset that I hadn't told her the truth about her sister and Tokyo, but I didn't have to.

I gave her what she'd wanted most.

Her life.

Her husband.

I did that shit. For her. But at this point, her words were like music to my ears. Whatever I felt for her, didn't compare to what I felt for Satin. I knew that now. And I also knew forgetting about Lava was probably the best thing for me to do.

Forgetting about her would help me focus.

I sat my phone in my lap and made a U-turn.

Carla's trip to see West was coincidental, according to Lava. That still didn't mean she was in the clear.

My phone started to vibrate.

At the sight of the number, I immediately knew who it was.

Pops.

I'd had Hamid pick me up a new phone, but I kept the same number just in case Satin called it. She and Pops were the only ones who had this number, so I always knew that if it was ringing it was one of them.

In this case, I wished it had been Satin.

I hesitated.

"Where are you?" he murmured once I put the phone to my ear.

"Washington."

"Cool, me too. You and Satin ready to go? It's hot. Real hot! I've been laying low, but it's time for us to move."

Pops is still in Washington?

And damn!

He didn't have Satin.

"The news said they picked you up…"

"Come on, you knew they wouldn't be able to hold me for too long. There's always a weak link. It took me no time to find it," Pops said. "It was nothing a little money couldn't handle. At least to get me out of their custody. Now, getting out of the country… I should've never come here in the first place. As you know, I only come when there's a problem. I let my guard down. Caesar created a problem…but it was all to set me up."

Caesar was a man Pops did business with here and there. He was the reason why Pops asked me to kill Dedrick in the first place. The hit was as a favor to him.

"That snake had been playing me the whole time. Running game on me for what, seven years? He never wanted Dedrick dead. As a matter of fact, he works with him… Well, he used to. Caesar, or whatever his real name is, is dead now. Once I turned one of his little buddies, I had them to shoot him in the back of his head. They sure as hell didn't put that on T.V. though, did they?"

Pops talked for a little while longer, and I felt like I'd played myself. I had Pops all wrong. He was completely normal. He was acting like himself. Pops didn't seem to have a malicious thought about me at all. I'd been tripping all along.

Pops simply said he tried not to make contact because he didn't know who was listening or watching. And with all the heat on him, more than anything, he hadn't wanted Satin anywhere near him. Not until he figured out his next, best, and safest move.

And now, he was ready.

"They grilled me for hours. They wanted you and Satin too, but I knew they weren't going to catch you. I knew she would be your main concern. I knew you would protect her and keep her safe. I am surprised you are still in the States though. But I planned for it. With all the heat on us, I couldn't be sure if you would take the risk of trying to get on a plane or not, but I have it all worked out. I'm going to text you an address. You and Satin meet me there. Where is she? Let me speak to her."

I'd been hoping he'd had her all along and had taken her to safety. Clearly, that wasn't the case.

"Pops…I don't know where she is."

"What do you mean you don't *know*?"

"I went by her apartment one day and she was gone. It was right before they arrested you and started putting my face all over the news. I thought maybe you had her."

"Why the fuck would I have her?" Pops yelled.

"Maybe you had a feeling something was about to go down and scooped her up. Took her to safety before I could. All I know is when I went by to get her she was wasn't there. I thought maybe you'd beat me to the punch."

I was lying some, but I knew he couldn't tell.

Pop breathed heavily. I knew how he felt about Satin, so I knew finding out she was missing was going to rock his world. I also knew he would move mountains to help me find her. "She's your wife. But she's *my* daughter. Find her, Kemp. Now!"

I wasn't scared of Pops.

I hadn't been for years. I would kill him if I had to.

If he didn't get someone to kill me first.

I'll admit it, I'd had Pops all wrong. From the looks of it, we were still on the same side. At least, for now. I could only imagine he would blame me, if I never found her, and then…

"I have looked everywhere for her. Even with all the attention and the money on my head, I've still been looking for her day and night."

"You should've never lost her in the first place," Pops interrupted. "How you find her isn't my problem. Just find her. I'll stay here. I'll stay hidden for a few more days. Think, son. And if you need me to make a call, I will. If it'll help you find her. Keep your phone on you. And the next time I call you, Satin better be with you."

And then he hung up.

~***~

TOKYO

"Thank you. Have a nice day," I said to the cashier.

I hurried out of the store, though I wasn't sure why. I walked fast, as though someone was chasing me.

After the shooting, I drove away and I've been driving ever since.

I'd been driving in circles, staying from hotel to hotel, trying to figure out what was next. Trying to figure out where I wanted to be.

I'd driven all the way to California but remembered the heartache I endured there, so I was on the road again, heading down south.

I hadn't seen my face on the news or anything, but I'd definitely stopped the wedding. I'd shot Drea and Lava, according to the story online.

Neither of them had died and the police were still asking for any information that could help them make an arrest.

I was surprised Drea hadn't given them my name.

She knew it was me.

She knew I'd shot her.

And she knew she'd deserved it.

I'd checked her social media pages. She'd apologized to the guests then she told everyone that she and Boris were going to take the shooting as a sign and part ways. They'd decided not to get married.

My heart was happy.

Drea had gotten what she'd deserved.

And hell, in a sense, so had Lava.

I wasn't sure if I should worry about Kemp coming after me. With everyone looking for him, I was probably the last thing on my mind. At least, that's what I was hoping. And if not, if there ever came a day where I had to face him again, so be it. I didn't have anything or anyone to live for anyway.

Instinctively, once I was in my car, I glanced back at the car seat that was still there. I couldn't bring myself to take it out.

I'd recently looked up George and his wife, and what did I see?

My son, Japan.

They'd renamed him George Jr.

He was proudly showing him off, and though everyone seemed to have questions, he just seemed happy to finally have a child.

I wanted him back.

In a way, I needed him back.

He was the only person, in the world I felt truly loved me. He missed me. I was sure he did. But not nearly as much as I missed him. I hadn't carried him in my womb, but he was a part of me. He was everything to me which was the only thing keeping me from going back to Virginia and making them *give him back* to me.

On the run, at least for now, I couldn't give him what he needed. I was sure Drea would eventually turn me in. Even if she didn't, I didn't have anywhere to go. I didn't have anyone to turn to, and I didn't want him to end up with no one if something happened to me.

So, despite the many times I'd wanted to turn around for him, I didn't.

A sudden knock on my car window startled me.

I rolled down the window.

Wait...

What is he...

"Excuse me, ma'am. The bottom of your dress is hanging out of the door," he said.

It was Boris.

The man that was supposed to marry Drea.

She'd had pictures of him all over her pages, so I knew what he looked like. I'd spent hours staring at him with hate and envy.

He was handsome, and he smiled at me.

"Thank you so much. It's way to chilly for this thing anyway, but I wanted to be comfortable," I opened the door and smiled back at him. "It looks like it's going to rain," I said, making small talk.

"Yeah, it does. I hope so. I love the rain."

"Me too."

He stared at me, as though he was waiting to see what I would say next. I didn't say anything.

"I'm Boris."

"I'm Tokyo."

I said. Immediately, regretting giving him my real name. Being as though he extended his hand, I concluded Drea probably never mentioned me.

Why would she?

Clearly, he didn't know a thing about me.

"Nice to meet you, Tokyo."

He glanced at the tons of bags I had in the backseat.

"Going on a trip?"

"I don't really know where I'm going. I just got up one day and decided I wanted to be somewhere else. I wanted to start over."

He chuckled. "Tell me about it. I'm somewhat doing the same thing. I lived in Virginia. My life, uh, took an unexpected turn. I was supposed to be taking a job in Atlanta. Instead, after... Anyway, I ended up taking another job offer all the way in Mississippi so that's where I'm headed," he said.

"Mississippi. I've never been to Mississippi."

Boris licked his lips at me.

"It may be a nice place to start over. What you think?"

"Maybe."

What are the odds of me running into Boris, the same man Drea was going to marry to forget about me?

I chuckled aloud.

Life is crazy, isn't it?

"So, do you want to grab a bite to eat and talk about what life will be like in Mississippi?" He was flirting. I allowed it.

"Sure. If there is where you're going, maybe there is where I need to be."

Boris beamed. "Oh, okay. See, now we're talking. A woman that just goes for it, huh? I like it. We only live once, right?"

"Right."

I could tell he was in a vulnerable state.

Probably after everything that happened with Drea. He was probably sad, lonely, and disappointed.

Good.

I mean, hooking up with Boris was a hell of a way to get back at Drea.

Why hadn't I thought about getting close to Boris before instead of begging her to remember her words and promises to me?

All along, I should've been barking up the *Boris tree*.

A few minutes later I was following him as he drove slowly down the street, plotting on how I was going to make Boris fall in love with me.

By no means did I deserve a happy ending after all I'd done, but I wanted one. I needed one. I needed something to finally go right for me.

And if it all blew up in my face at the end, I would accept my fate. But for now…with Boris…it's a date!

Goodbye, Drea. Goodbye, Lava. Goodbye, West. And everything else back in Virginia.

Hello, Boris and Mississippi! Maybe this time little Ms. Tokyo had found herself a winner!

~***~

LAVA

"I do."

West smiled as the preacher spoke.

"By the power invested in me, I now pronounce you husband and wife…again. Please, kiss your bride."

Everyone cheered as West and I kissed each other.

We'd renewed our vows.

Drea had left for Atlanta and told mama to find something to do with all the stuff she'd bought for her wedding. Mama was just going to give it all away until West had an idea.

In front of everyone, he got down on one knee and asked me to marry him. *Again.* He said the past few years had been rough but renewing our vows would really give us a fresh start.

And so, that's just what we did.

I was still so full of anger and I wasn't too fond of using Drea's stuff, with her evil ass, but at least she'd been good for something.

"I love you," West said.

"Always."

"And forever," he said back.

We faced the crowd and headed down the small steps.

I smiled genuinely as we headed out the church. For reasons unknown, I started to look around once outside.

I was looking for him.

Kemp.

I wondered if he was somewhere watching me.

I hadn't heard from him again so maybe he was gone. Maybe.

"Hey, you okay?" West asked.

I beamed at him. "Never better."

We greeted everyone then made our way to the reception space.

"I'm so glad this shit is over," Thea said, approaching me. She'd been my spur of the moment maid of honor. Trying to pull everything off in just a few days drove her crazy!

But we got it done, and everything was beautiful. "Is that him? The one that caused all of the trouble between Janay and Declora?" she asked as she eyed Declora's wedding date.

"Yep, that's him."

"You think she puts her finger in his ass?" Thea questioned. I snickered.

"Eww, please, I don't even want to think about it."

Thea and I laughed from a good, healthy place.

"Well, I'm just glad the two of them were able to move past it. Y'all already lost one sister. I'm sure neither of you want to lose another."

Drea got out the hospital, and she left town, almost immediately.

From what she told mama, she wasn't sure when or if she would ever come back. But she invited mama to come and see her anytime she wanted or needed to. She told her all she had to do was ask.

Drea told everyone goodbye, except me.

We still weren't speaking but one night I'd decided to text her.

I told her I was sorry.

I told her I forgave her, even though it wasn't all the way true. I was still mad as hell at her, but for the most part, I just wanted to move on. I just wanted my life to go back to how it used to be.

Drea never responded to my text.

"And neither of you are going to turn Tokyo in?"

"Who?"

Thea laughed.

I just wanted to forget about Tokyo too.

Drea didn't give the police her name.

I guess she felt as though she'd brought it all onto herself. As for me, I'm not exactly sure why I didn't turn her in. I didn't owe Tokyo a damn thing.

But we all had done some fucked up things. We all contributed to the hell we'd been going through. I guess I figured if I was lucky enough to get a second chance at life…if I could still have a happy ending…

I guess, maybe, for some strange reason, I hoped that somewhere she could too.

"Umph, look at my sexy ass husband." Thea licked her lips at Ying as he danced around with their daughter.

"Girl, ain't shit sexy about Ying," I laughed at her.

"Bitch, please! My man is all of that and a bag of chips! You wish he was yours. Too bad. He's all mine!" Thea grinned and headed to join them. I smiled at them and then I looked around the room.

Everyone was happy.

This is happiness.

This is peace.

This was life…without Kemp.

West and I made eye contact.

He walked over to me and immediately reached for my hand. I took it after shaking away all of my worries.

I was going to be okay.

We were going to be okay.

And life was going to be better than ever.

And after vowing to forget the past and all my pain…and after forgiving myself for something I'd *recently* done that I knew I probably shouldn't have, I leaped into the arms of my husband and there was where I wanted to stay…

Forever.

~***~

SATIN

Oh God, help me! Help me get out of here!

~***~

KEMP

Somehow, I ended up at Satin's apartment again.

For the past few days, I'd just been sitting and watching the apartment building.

I'd spent a few of the other days trying to tap into a few resources now that I knew Pops wasn't working against me, but I still hadn't found anything.

I still hadn't found her.

Satin's car was still just sitting there. They hadn't towed it or anything. It was just there.

I hadn't seen any cops snooping around. That's what I'd been looking for. Maybe they were moving on or maybe they figured I had.

The apartments were brick, with an entrance in the front, and in the back. They had three floors, but both Satin and I had apartments on the first floor.

An old lady came out of the building with her dog. I wondered if I should wait for her to go back inside before trying to make a move.

I wasn't sure if Satin's stuff was still inside of the apartment, but I needed to see. If her stuff was still in there then maybe there was something I'd missed before.

I was desperate.

I'd checked into every possible lead, and I was still coming up with nothing. And with Pops breathing down my neck, it only made matters worse.

I was starting to believe that Lava was right.

Carla most likely didn't have anything to do with whatever had happened to Satin. She seemed to be moving on. She was seeing someone new, and every time I saw her she had this big ass grin on her face. She didn't look like a woman who was hiding something...or someone.

Dedrick was M.I.A.

I hadn't see him.

I didn't know where he was.

But I knew that he was somewhere.

Watching. Waiting.

It had been a while now since Satin had been gone. I hadn't told Pops the whole truth about when she'd disappeared, but he didn't care about the specifics anyway.

He just wanted her home.

He was already gone. He left me behind to find her, but he was checking in almost hourly, only to be disappointed every time he called.

He and Satin's mother had left Cairo.

He knew they'd always be looking for him there so, for now, he was in Paris. With everything out about him, what he did, and what he was involved with, he was thinking about giving it all up.

That's what he said.

I didn't believe him.

Checking the bullets in my new gun, I pulled my hood over my face and got out the car.

The lady that was walking her dog started to head back in my direction just as I was about to enter the apartment building.

"I wouldn't go in there if I were you."

I stopped.

"We never spoke, but I lived right next door to her. A police officer is there. He's been there for a while now. He never leaves. I'm assuming he's waiting for one of you."

Peeking at her, I could see how old she was.

"I saw you helping her move in and a time or two after that. Then I never saw you again until I saw you on the news. Did you do what they said you did?"

I didn't answer her.

"Well, she hasn't been back here if that's why you're here. And if I were you, young man, I wouldn't come back here either. I don't need their money. I'm eighty-three years old. Don't have much use for it. But trust me, if someone else sees you..."

I turned around, still silent, preparing to go back to my car.

"Were you one of her lovers too?"

"No, she's my sister."

The old lady walked towards the door. "Ah, okay. That makes sense. Well, your sister sure did get around. I'm not sure what all the fuss is about. I'm sure she ran off with one of her men. For a while, I saw one fella. The black one. The one that keeps coming by here. And then one day I caught the back of her as she was leaving with another fella. Now that I think about it, that may be the last time I saw her. It was her though. I could tell from her behind. I used to be stacked like that back in the day. Those were the good ole days."

Her words caught my attention, so I took a chance and asked a question.

"You said the last time you saw her. Do you remember what the guy looked like that she was with?"

"No, I only saw the back of him. They weren't coming out this way. They were going out the back way. I was coming into the building, so I couldn't see his face."

"What could you see?"

She thought for a moment.

She rambled on and on, but her last comment was all that I needed.

I put two and two together.

It had to be him.

I had to be right.

Finally, I knew exactly who had my wife.

~***~

SATIN

"Kiss me."

I turned up my nose at him.

"When are you going to stop making things so difficult? Just stop fighting it," he said.

I'd lost count of how long I'd been here.

I'd hoped Kemp would find me by now, but I was sure he didn't have a clue as to where I was.

He came closer to me and kissed my lips without my permission.

"Could you at least take this chain off my ankles?"

He smiled.

"No. Would you rather me chain your wrists?"

I shook my head.

I was going to kill him. One day he was going to slip up and I was going to kill him.

"Go on and pee so I can empty the bucket before I leave.

Keeping my eyes on him, I squatted over the bucket.

I was so ready to get out of here!

He stared at me as the urine clanked against the bottom of the bucket. And then he passed me the roll of tissue.

He was crazy!

I could tell by the look in his eyes that soon dressing me up in lipstick and lingerie wasn't going to be enough.

He was going to want more...

Even though he'd already had *more* before.

His phone started to ring just as he picked up the bucket of waste.

"It's my wife. I guess I should be getting home."

He was already home.

At least, I think.

I knew for a fact that I was in some kind of basement or something. I'd tried screaming, almost every day, once he was gone, but no one ever seemed to hear me.

Maybe I was somewhere else.

I couldn't be sure.

He had me chained at the ankles to a big pipe. The pipe came up out of the basement floor and went all the way up the wall. I'd tried pulling at it and kicking at it. I'd tried everything to get out of there, but nothing worked.

I was stuck down there.

He came to visit me every day with food and water.

And every day, he brought me a new piece of lingerie.

At first, I thought that it was about money.

Or maybe even about revenge.

But it didn't take me long to figure out that this wasn't about either of those things.

This was all about me.... all because of me.

Because he loved me. At least, that's what he'd said.

He told me that he'd never done anything like this before. And strangely, I believed him.

"It's just you," he'd said to me. "It's just---you."

His phone stopped ringing. Of course, he never answered it. He knew that I would scream.

"I'll be back. And don't worry. You won't be chained up like this much longer. I'm trying to figure everything out. I just needed a little time."

He grabbed the bucket and then he walked up the stairs. And then he turned out the lights.

I sat there in the dark.

"Kemp, baby, please save me."

This was me paying for my sins.

My actions coming back to bite me in the ass.

I was facing my worst nightmare.

And my worst nightmare was…

Ying.

Ying. The husband of Lava's cousin, Thea, was my kidnapper. And at one point in time, he was also one of my *fools*. It was many years ago and before he was married.

Ying was the third.

The third man that I'd been *with*, while married to Kemp. I was assigned to him. My "job" was the same as always and that was to get information out of him. And during the process, just as I'd done with all of the others, I'd pretended to fall in love with him and I made him fall in love with me too.

And then…

I disappeared.

No, Kemp hadn't tried to kill him.

His role wasn't important enough. At least, not back then. Back then, my father was actually after the man that Ying worked for at the time. Ying was his second in command, but my father said he was the easier target.

And after months of being everything that he wanted me to be, Ying started to trust me, vent to me, and tell me things about his job that I wasn't supposed to know. I would also snoop on his computer and go through his phone after I'd *put it on him* and put him to sleep.

I would then take the information back to my father and he would use it to his benefit.

Finally, my father told me that my job was over. And without telling Ying goodbye or giving him closure, one day, I was just gone.

And then he saw me again with Kemp.

Back when I first started the *job*, to seduce George, I saw Ying coming out of a store one day. I told Kemp that he was in Virginia. He'd been living in Connecticut when I'd *played* him years ago, and I'd hoped that I wouldn't run into him.

I never did.

The entire time in Virginia, I managed to avoid Ying.

Even after Thea slapped me that day in the nail salon, knowing that she was Ying's wife was the only thing that had stopped me from showing up at her house and getting my *lick* back.

But then, Ying was referred to my father and to Kemp.

Of course, Ying hadn't known anything about what my father had put me up to all those years ago. He didn't know that my father was the reason I'd entered his life only to use him and then leave. Ying's contact only knew that my father had a way of making problems disappear…for a fee and usually for a little something extra in return.

And since Ying had the money and a few secrets on the men at the top of the Fortune 500 company that he'd worked for, my father gave Kemp the okay to provide the service.

I was going to leave before their meeting that day, but Ying and Thea were early. And so, he saw me, standing next to Kemp and we both pretended as though we'd never met.

I remembered him staring at me as though he'd seen a ghost. As though he couldn't believe that I was really there.

Ying had never seen me with Kemp and Kemp had never had any prior interaction with Ying. He'd only watched him from a distance while I was with him.

So, as far as Ying knew I'd met Kemp after him.

Still, after the initial shock, Ying seemed okay. Thea eyed me sarcastically, the whole time, but other than that the meeting went fine. The transaction went through and Ying's problems were handled as promised.

Ying was a very smart man. I'd always known that. And his talents didn't stop at money. Apparently, he knew how to kidnap someone without leaving a trace too. And I had a feeling that he was going to get away with it.

Ying told me that ever since the day, the day he'd first saw me again, he craved me. He wanted me. He said that keeping his composure around his wife and around Kemp was the hardest thing that he'd ever had to do.

He said he remembered the times that we shared.

He remembered the love that he had for me and that he was obsessed with me and my beauty.

That part was obvious.

And since I'd been locked up in the basement, Ying did the craziest shit like lick my face, and sniff my hair. Sometimes he would smell my urine and force me to let him paint my toes.

He'd lost his damn mind!

Literally!

Ying expressed that he'd just gotten into town on the same day that I'd popped up at Lava's house and threatened her to stay away from Kemp. He'd said that he hadn't told Thea that he was in Virginia. He was going to surprise her.

Ying said as he rode by Lava's house he spotted me walking to my car. Even with my hair a different color and fake eyes, he'd said that he knew that it was me.

So, instead of going home he made a U-turn and followed me back to Washington.

For days, he watched me.

He said he told Thea that he was still on the ship just so he could follow me around and obsess over me.

He even knew that Kemp was in town. He'd watched me go across the parking lot one night. And then he said the next day he drove right by Kemp, without Kemp even noticing.

Ying said that he was jealous.

Jealous of Kemp.

Because he had me.

So, he started making plans to take me from him.

And then that day, the day that I was supposed to meet Kemp at the airport, Ying knocked on my door.

I looked out of the peep hole before opening it.

I knew who he was. I was shocked to see him.

Confused.

On a *normal* day, I would've never opened the door. I was rushing. I was panicking. I was distracted with everything that was going on and I wasn't thinking straight.

I was in a hurry.

And…I opened the door.

Ying said all of five words to me before attacking me.

I'd tried to fight him off, but it was to no surprised that he knew a few moves. And he'd come prepared. He pulled out a gun. I'd tried to make it to my gun, the one I kept in my purse, but he grabbed me by my hair and put the gun to my back.

He forced me to leave everything behind and we walked out of the back entrance of the apartment building where his car was waiting for me. He told me to get into the backseat and just as I was about to say something, with the end of the gun, he knocked me out cold.

And then I woke up in this basement.

It wasn't until I'd been here for over a day that he came back and told me what he wanted with me.

He told me that he wanted me…forever.

I'd laughed in his face, but he'd meant his words.

Later, Ying told me that I was lucky that he'd taken me when he had because Kemp's face was all over the news. He also said that my father had been arrested.

In his mind, he actually thought that he'd saved me.

There wasn't a T.V. or anything in the basement so, I could only take his word for what was going on. I knew that it had some truth to it because Dedrick had warned me.

I guess he really had been trying to save me.

Ying told me that he'd called in a tip to tell the police to watch the apartment building for Kemp. He wanted Kemp in jail, but I knew that he wouldn't succeed.

Kemp is smart.

He won't get caught. No matter what Ying tries.

Ying said that he'd been following Kemp around whenever he could. He said after he took me he kept his eyes open for Kemp and his car in Virginia. And then one day he saw him.

He said that he'd followed Kemp to Lava's a few times, but Kemp never got out of the car. Ying said that he would just sit there. He asked why I'd gone to see Lava that day. I didn't tell him, but he figured that Kemp was watching Lava's house, hoping that I would come back there again. Obviously, he wasn't aware of Lava's and Kemp's past fling, but it made me wonder what the hell

Kemp was doing and why he was watching Lava's house in the first place.

He knew I wasn't there.

Why was he wasting time?

Instead of using it to look for me?

Ying bragged that Kemp would never figure out that he had me and I was starting to believe him. Kemp could find anyone, but he couldn't seem to find me.

I exhaled loudly as I tried to get comfortable on top of the stack of blankets.

I'd been putting my training to use and trying to get inside of Ying's head. That's how I'd found out that he wasn't mistreated, neglected or raised by crazy people.

He was just crazy…about me.

I asked him about Thea.

He told me that she was perfect for him.

He told me how much he loved her. So, I told him that what he was doing was going to hurt her. All he said was that he had a plan. He said that he could make her accept it.

Accept it?

Accept what?

Me?

As what?

Their other woman?

He kept saying that we would be leaving soon.

Where would we go?

Was Thea coming with us?

She couldn't know what he was up to.

Right?

You just never know what people are into these days. Or who they really are and what they are capable of.

Ying was proof of that.

I yanked at the chain in the dark.

It was a big, rusted chain, and it was heavy, and tight around both ankles. He'd wrapped it around one ankle, left a little chain, and then wrapped it around the other. I could stand up and somewhat shuffle around, but I couldn't go too far. Ying made sure that there was nothing within my reach, though there wasn't much of anything down there anyway. There was a box in a corner far away from me and that was about it. And when he fed me or gave me something to drink, it was always on a paper plate and out of a paper cup. Most of the time he brought me pizza. If I never ate a slice of pizza again---it would be too soon!

He even removed the wires from the bra cups before bringing it to me.

I closed my eyes.

I was going to die down here.

I was sure of it.

Unless Kemp saved me.

Come on Kemp...save me.

~***~

KEMP

I was trying to keep calm.

When the lady told me that she'd seen Satin leaving with a short, Asian or Chinese man, only one person came to my mind.

Ying.

He was the only Chinese man that she'd ever dealt with.

He was worth checking into.

Unless it was someone else.

I'll admit, he never crossed my mind. He was someone that I wouldn't suspect. We'd met and done a little business, but he seemed happy with Thea.

Why would he want Satin?

Sure, she'd played him in the past, but he wouldn't still be hung up on that.

Would he?

I'd come back to Virginia and I was watching the house that he and Thea shared. So far, nothing seemed out of the ordinary. Ying went home. He went to play golf. He went to visit a few men in suits. He took food to what I found out to be his mother's house. He would even take her outside and walk her around. She seemed old. Maybe even blind or something.

There was nothing about him that would make me think that he was the man that the old lady had seen with Satin. His body language and the smile that he wore on his face told me that I was probably barking up the wrong tree.

Still, I needed to be sure.

Ying came out of the house.

I saw Thea come out onto the porch. It was late evening, and she and Ying were arguing. She was going on and on about something and Ying kept trying to walk away from her.

Since I'd been back in Virginia, I'd forced myself to stay away from Lava, but I'd seen her earlier that day.

She'd come by Thea's house.

Our last conversation was sour, but I was doing what she'd asked me to do. I was letting her be. That was the best thing for her and for me.

I just wanted Satin back.

Ying had a bag in his hand.

He walked away from Thea and she disappeared into the house. Ying got into his car and before she came back outside, he drove away.

Cranking up, I prepared to follow him, but I stopped once I saw Thea running out of the house. She hopped into her car and sped down the road after him.

Lava had taken Thea's baby with her earlier that day. Thea must've known that all of this was coming.

Ying stopped at the stop sign once he saw Thea. And then he turned around. And so, did she.

What the hell are they doing?

They both came back home and Ying got back out of the car, without the bag, and Thea followed him back into their house all while screaming at the top of her lungs.

I cut the car off and waited.

And waited.

I didn't have anywhere else to go.

And then, around midnight, I saw Ying sneak out of the front door.

He tiptoed towards his car and barely shutting the driver's side door, he pulled off. I waited for him to make a right turn at the stop sign before I started to follow him.

I was surprised to see that he'd only gone about five minutes up the road---back to his mother's house.

Hmmm.

This was the first time that he'd gone there at night since I'd been following him around.

He got the bag out of the car, the one that he'd had earlier that day, and he headed for the front door.

Once he was inside, the lights flipped on and I waited to see what would happen next.

What is he doing?

I was damn sure going to find out!

Just as I reached for my new gun, I saw the lights and then another car swerved into Ying's mother's driveway.

Thea.

I laughed aloud.

She didn't miss a beat!

She got out of the car, half dressed, and hurried towards the front door. She knocked on it. And then she kicked it. Over and over again, but Ying never opened it.

She screamed at the top of her lungs and after standing on the porch for a little while, she got back into her car.

I waited for her to pull off, so I could get out, but she didn't. For a long time, she just sat there.

And so, I sat there too.

Eventually, the sun came up and just as birds started to chirp, through heavy eyes, I watched Thea get out of the car again. She walked back to the front door and she just stood there.

She didn't knock.

She didn't kick or scream.

She just stood there.

As though she knew Ying would be coming out of the house soon.

Finally, he opened the front door.

And Thea pushed past him and went inside.

Ying disappeared from the doorway and in a hurry, I got out of the car.

I ran across the street. I could hear them arguing as I approached the yard, but I didn't go towards the front door. I went around to the back instead.

Something about this situation was off.

Something was wrong.

I found the back door and went to work. I picked the lock in less than two minutes. With my gun still in my hand, slowly, I opened the door. I could hear Ying and Thea quarrelling, but they seemed to be far away.

I entered the house in what looked like the laundry room. Shutting the door behind me, I followed the voices until I reached the kitchen.

"Shit!" I whispered.

The little old woman, Ying's mother, walked right in front of me, but she didn't see me.

And being that she didn't turn around, I didn't think that she'd heard me either.

She stuck her cane out in front of her, making her way to the refrigerator.

She *was* blind.

She opened it and after feeling around for a second, she grabbed a bottle of juice and with her cane guiding her, she walked back by me and down the hall to another room.

And that's when I heard the sound.

Boom!

It was a gunshot.

Cautiously, I tried to find where the noise had come from. I seemed to be going around in circles, until I came to a small door, at the far end of the house. A door that led into something that looked like a basement.

I knew once I went down the stairs, there was no turning back. They would know that I was there.

And someone has a gun.

I didn't know what I was walking into, but I walked down the steps anyway.

And that's when I saw...

~***~

THEA

I shot him.

And then I just stood there as Ying struggled to breathe.

"I hate you! I fucking hate you!"

My inner voice screamed, but I couldn't seem to say the words aloud.

Unexpectedly, my mind started to replay the last couple of weeks.

Ying and I had been bumping heads like crazy, here lately. When he first came home, I could tell that he really didn't want to be here. He seemed anxious, or awkward, as though he'd gotten used to living on the water. As though he wanted to go back. I could tell that something wasn't right, but he'd tried to hide it. He'd tried to be content.

At first, we were having sex and getting along and then one day, everything changed. He stopped talking to me. He stopped touching me. Once, he'd come into our bedroom and I had my ass up in the air, waiting for him.

Still, he declined.

He said that he was tired.

Tired of what?

Ying ain't never turned down this pussy!

Right then and there, I was convinced that there was something that he wasn't telling me.

And then he started finding reasons to get away from me. He acted like he didn't want to be at home.

After following him a few times, I found out that he was going to his mama's house every day.

But why?

I asked him about it, and he said that he was going over there to check on her, and to sit and talk with her.

Really?

First of all, the woman was as old as Egyptian pyramids, blind as a bat, and partially deaf; she couldn't hear a thing, unless she had on her hearing aids so, what could he possibly be talking to her about?

And for hours? Every goddamn day!

And the fact that he'd fired her nurse, and sent his sisters, who helped take care of her, on some surprise vacation didn't sit well with me either.

Something was up with him.

So, I asked him.

Over and over again, but he kept saying that he was fine and that he could spend time with his mama if he wanted to. I tried to be understanding, I really did.

But as the days continued to roll by, he got weirder and weirder and I got madder and madder!

We started arguing, all the time, but no matter what I said he wouldn't break. And then when I felt him creep out of bed, in the middle of the night, I knew that it was something more.

So, I got up.

I knew that if he'd gone to his mother's house then it was something over there that I didn't know about. Something that he didn't want me to see.

And I was right.

After waiting for hours, once he opened the door, I'd come into the house fussing and demanding answers. I checked in every bedroom. I told him that I was going to divorce his raggedy ass if he didn't tell me what was going on and still, he'd tried to act all innocent.

Until I approached the basement door.

He stood in front of it.

I tried to fight past him, but he kept telling me to wait.

"Wait. Wait. Wait. Let me talk to you first," he'd said. And then he asked me. "Can we go away?"

"Go away where?" I'd asked him.

"Anywhere. Back to the water. Just away."

I screamed at him and told him that we could if he moved away from the door.

He hesitated. "Can we take her with us?"

Her?

Who the fuck is her?

Ying moved away from the door and I hurried down the basement stairs. And that's when I saw her.

Satin.

Chained.

Wearing lingerie and lipstick.

Lying on top of blankets as though they were a bed.

Ying hurried down the stairs and tried to explain. Of course, Lava told me that Kemp told her that Satin was missing, but never in a million years did I think my goddamn husband was responsible for it!

Why?

Why take her when he had me?

Immediately, Satin started to plead. She begged me to tell him to let her go.

The whole time Ying had been carrying a bag on his arm. The same bag that he'd been carrying out of the house the day before, but it looked lighter. It looked empty. As though he'd had things in it to give to her.

I'd glanced down at it. It was half open, so I pulled at it and he allowed it. I started to fumble around inside of it.

Inside of the bag was his mother's hearing aids, whip cream…and his gun.

Nervous, I'd pulled my hand out of the bag and he hung the bag on the old wooden rail of the stairs beside of me.

I'd stared at him in pure disgust.

"How could you do something like this?" I'd asked him.

"She started it. Years ago. When she seduced me." He blamed Satin, but I didn't have a clue what the fuck he was talking about.

"I just had to have her---again. I don't know what came over me. I want her Thea. And you. You said that you wanted to try something new, with me."

"Yes, with someone who was *willing*! Not with a fucking hostage, you damn fool!" I'd started to cry. "How could you? This is so fucked up!" I was in disbelief.

"It's not all that bad, baby. Let's just go. We can take her with us and it will be just the four of us. You, me, her, and our baby. Look at her, she's so beautiful. She's the girl from both of our fantasies. The type of girl that you said that you would try with me. Only you didn't know that she was real. And that I'd had her---once upon a time. Come on baby. You're my ride or die," Ying pleaded.

He was right.

I was.

I was his ride or die. But on this ride…I was getting the hell off!

In that moment, all that mattered was that he'd called her beautiful, as though he no longer seen the beauty in me. All I heard was how bad he wanted her, as though I wasn't enough anymore.

And full of rage, embarrassment, betrayal, and a whole lot of other shit, I glanced at the bag, and remembering the gun inside of it. And while Ying continued to plead and beg me to *keep* her, I reached inside of the bag, grabbed the gun and then…I pulled the trigger.

My eyes started to flutter and the sound of the footsteps behind me caused me to look back at the stairs.

Kemp?

What the hell is he doing here?

He was holding a gun.

I was still holding Ying's gun. Tight in my hands.

"Give me the gun Thea," I heard Kemp say.

"Kemp?" She spoke up.

He took his attention off of me at the sound of her voice.

"Kemp," she sobbed.

Have you ever seen beauty in the midst of a storm?

The way that Kemp reacted once he saw Satin was something out of a movie. He'd been holding a gun, but he pushed it towards me and hell, not knowing what else to do, I grabbed it.

Kemp started to cry---like real tears and shit, all the way down to his knees and then he crawled towards her.

"Kemp," she repeated until he reached her.

He pulled her close to him and held her as she started to wail. It was one of the most beautiful, yet tragic things that I'd ever seen.

It was love. It was pain.

Pain that my twisted ass husband had caused.

"I knew that you would find me. I knew that you would come for me. I knew it. I knew it."

For a while, I was invisible to them.

Kemp focused on trying to free Satin's ankles from the chains and finally, I turned my attention back to the man who had put them there.

Ying's eyes were still open, but he was gone.

My husband, my love, my *devil*---was dead.

~***~

SATIN

He was already dead, but Kemp told me to shoot him anyway. He told me to take my power back. The power that mentally, Ying had stolen from me.

With my ankles free, Kemp asked Thea to give him both of the guns.

She did.

And then Kemp reached one of them to me.

"Shoot him."

I obeyed him and squeezed the trigger.

And then I squeezed it again. And again. Until it was empty.

Slowly, Kemp removed the gun from my hands and then he got busy. He said that he was going to get rid of Ying's body and the guns…as a thank you to Thea.

Thea didn't thank him or say anything at all. She was quiet as she headed up the stairs.

Kemp told me to sit at the bottom of them while he made a phone call for help.

It was over. My worst nightmare was dead.

I'd been scared.

Worried.

After so long, I wasn't sure what would happen to me.

All of this was my fault. It was all because of me. Because of my father. And because of my so-called job.

But I was done.

As God is my witness, I was finished!

I looked behind me as I took a seat on the stairs.

Through my tears, I saw Thea standing there.

She was at the top. Stuck. Maybe she was in shock.

"Go home, Thea. And never tell anyone what happened here. Don't tell anyone what you did, or that Ying is dead."

Thea didn't reply and after a few more seconds, she simply walked away.

"Thank you," I mumbled. Thea had saved the day.

~***~

DEDRICK

"You okay, boss?"

I nodded.

I was worried about how my legs would hold up on the beach.

It had been months now since Kemp shot me and since he'd fallen off of the grid, but I had him in my sight.

Him and his wife.

Months ago, Lava, the woman that he'd been acquainted with, called in with a tip. I'd called her once before, trying to get information out of her, but she'd lied. She said that she hadn't seen or spoken to him.

And then she called in. My assistant took her call.

She told her that Kemp had mentioned running off to the Cayman Islands, once he found Satin.

And there they were.

I'd told my assistant to keep quiet about the tip and that when I was able, I would handle him. I'd wanted to arrest this fool myself.

I hadn't planned to bother Satin.

I was just going to arrest Kemp and let her go, but watching her, holding his hand and kissing him wasn't easy for me.

Kemp was right.

I'd known exactly who she was and still, I fell for her. I'd put everything on the line to warn her, to save her, but it was clear that she never felt a thing for me.

It wasn't real. And what they had---was.

So, I was taking her in, right along with her man.

I gave my boys the eye and we moved in.

The beach was crowded, even though it was obvious that a storm was on its way. The wind blew wildly, but everyone seemed at peace.

We were about to cause a scene.

They stood there, staring out at the ocean as we walked up behind them. I'd had a team of five men to come with me and they stood beside me as I started to speak.

"Kemp and Satin, or whatever your real last names are, you are under arrest. You have the right to remain silent. Anything that you say…"

As my men approached them holding handcuffs, Satin looked at me, but strangely Kemp kept his eyes on her. And then he spoke to her just as the thunder sounded above our heads.

"Baby…Until death do us part?" He asked her.

She smiled as they put her hands behind her back.

"Until death do us part."

At that very moment, she took her eyes off of me and before my guys could fully put the handcuffs on either of them, they both started to run.

They ran towards the ocean and my men started to scream and pulled out their guns.

"Hold your fire! Hold your fire!"

They were both already in the water, swimming, as two of my men ran in behind them.

Thunder roared just as the rain started to fall.

Until death do us part?

They'd planned this.

They'd rather die, drown, than to be taken in.

I couldn't say that I was surprised.

For a while, I could see them, swimming further and further out to sea.

And then I saw the wave.

My focus was on Satin as the wave crashed into both of them. I waited to see her, but only Kemp came up to the surface.

Where is Satin?

Where is she?

I watched him as he went back underwater. He was looking for her. My men were struggling to catch up to him. Kemp came up from the water and looked back at them, before looking around for Satin again. And then with more waves coming in, he went back underwater, but this time---he never came back up.

I kept my eyes on the water.

I saw my men struggling and finally, they turned around. They started to swim back towards the shore.

Still, I waited.

I waited for Kemp or Satin to resurface, but they never did. And after almost an hour of just standing there, watching, soak and wet from the rain, there was only one last thing to be said.

The one and only, Kemp and Satin…were dead.

~***~

One Month Later

KEMP

"Excuse me, sexy, but my friend over there would like to buy you a drink," she said to me.

I smiled at her as I pointed at Satin.

"I'm sorry, but I'm with that sexy thing right there. And I don't think she would like that too much. Do you?"

The three women snarled at Satin and then walked away.

I turned my attention back to my phone.

I laughed aloud seeing that Tokyo had married Boris, the man that Drea had been planning to marry.

How the fuck did that happen?

Tokyo was smiling. She seemed happy, but she was going to lose it once she found out that Boris…was gay.

The pictures that I'd found of him and his lover were from a long time ago, but I wouldn't doubt that something was still there. Maybe he liked both. Or maybe marrying a woman was his cover-up. Either way, if the truth about him ever came out, Tokyo was in for a hell of a surprise.

Drea was back home in Virginia.

She'd had some kind of outburst in the middle of a courtroom, back in Atlanta, according to the papers. She went into a rant and screamed at voices that she said were in her head. She'd had to be sedated. I couldn't be sure, but maybe she was losing her mind. I tell you, guilt is a parasite and it will eat at you over time.

No one understood that better than me.

Thea and her baby were doing well.

She'd done everything I'd told her to do.

That day, I called in a favor from Pops. I told him that I'd found Satin, and that the man who had taken her was dead. And then I told him that I needed him to send people that he could still trust to help get rid of the body.

He did.

I remember going upstairs to check and see what Ying's mother was doing, before help arrived. She couldn't see or hear anything, but I'd checked in on her anyway, only to find her sitting in a rocking chair, in her bedroom…dead.

She and her son died on the same day.

But only one of them would get a proper burial.

It took us a while to clean up the basement.

We couldn't leave any traces of blood, Satin, Thea or me behind. We had to move Ying's body, dispose of it, get rid of his car, all while making sure that no one noticed.

We got it done though.

That sick motherfucker had gotten just what he'd deserved.

And then on our way out, I stopped by Thea's house.

I told her it was done. I told her what to do next. I told her to report Ying missing, but I assured her that he would never be found. And I told her that if she did exactly what I told her to do, nothing would ever come back to her. And then I told her that the best thing for her to do was to try and forget about what she'd done. I told her that we all had secrets. I told her that she'd done the right thing.

And then I told her to move on.

And from the looks of it she had.

It didn't look as though she was seeing anyone, yet, but she was definitely enjoying the fuck out of what used to be Ying's money.

Just for the hell of it, I looked into Cheyenne and George to see how things were going with the baby. I was surprised to see that George's wife had left him. And the day after she'd changed her status to "Single" online, George was in a picture with the baby, and some other chick---who somewhat looked like Satin.

I placed my phone in my pocket and grabbed our food.

I smiled at Satin as I headed in her direction.

We were now in Peru.

And no one knew where we were.

No one knew that we were still alive.

Not even Pops.

That day, in the Cayman Islands, Dedrick showing up wasn't expected---but I couldn't say that we were surprised. I'd known that I would probably run into him again. So, Satin and I had discussed what to do, just in case.

I'd always told her that the water was the way out if that day ever came. If we were close enough to it.

Learning to swim had been one of the many things that Satin's father had us to learn. We could both swim, damn good, and we could stay underwater from six to eight minutes at a time.

That day, as we ran towards the water, I told her once she went down, not to come back up. I told her to swim

313

towards the crowd to our right. It had the most people. I told her not come up until she absolutely had to. Six to eight minutes of swimming would get us far enough away from Dedrick and into a crowd of people to blend in. And then after taking a quick breath we could go right back underwater again.

When I saw the wave coming, I told her to go under.

And it worked.

The rain helped us out even more.

When I came back up, I pretended to be looking for her. I knew that he would be watching, but with his men closing in, I knew that I had to get away, so I went under and the next time that I came out of the water, I was behind a small boat of people.

They were getting soaked from the rain and drinking, and none of them even noticed me.

I was quite a bit away from Dedrick and the shore. And then I looked around for Satin. We'd also discussed what to do if we were ever separated, so I knew if I didn't spot her that she would follow the plan.

But I saw her.

She was even further away than I was.

And after taking a deep breath I headed in her direction.

Tired, breathless, finally, we made it far enough away to where we felt safe enough to get out of the water and execute our escape plan.

And now…we were free.

We saw the story about us on the news.

"Fugitives drowned. Suicide"

That's what they'd called it.

They'd performed this big search for our bodies that of course, they never found.

Although Dedrick reported that they had.

We knew that Pops would never believe that we'd drowned, but Dedrick's lie actually helped us completely disappear. We had no idea whose bodies Dedrick were claiming to have found, but they weren't ours. And we knew that with Pops in hiding he wouldn't be able to verify anything or go and see the bodies for himself.

So, he'd had to take Dedrick's word for it.

He had to believe that we were dead---especially since we hadn't reach out to him. He'd known we were in the Cayman Islands, but he didn't know that I'd had some other things in the works for us.

Satin and I hid for a little over a week and then once I had everything ready for us, we took a private plane, curtesy of my South American connection, and settled in Peru.

Satin talked about missing her father and mother, but she knew that letting them think that we were dead was for the best. She'd said that as long as we had each other, that was all that mattered.

"Thank you, baby," Satin said. "It looks like you have an audience." She smiled at me with her beautiful, dark, curly hair blowing in the wind. Her hair was growing, and she was glowing.

Satin is pregnant.

It'd happened one night underneath the stars, on the beaches of the Cayman Islands. I knew exactly what I was doing. I'd wanted to. And even though I wasn't sure of our future, I knew that I wanted her and a child with her in it.

She was everything to me.

Although I'd had to *lose* her and get completely over Lava to see it.

Lava ratted me out.

I knew that it was because of her that Dedrick had found us. She was the only person that I'd told where we would go once I found Satin.

I couldn't blame her.

She was mad at me. At least, I'm sure she was when she'd told Dedrick my plans. I could accept that. Especially since her actions, in the end, also helped us.

Lava selling me out was the reason why Satin and I could live the rest of our lives 100% free.

So, in the end, Lava's snitching ass was the real MVP.

****

THE END (Finale!!)

Join My Brand New Reading Group:

https://www.facebook.com/groups/pageswithbm/

Check out these books next:

Her 13th Husband: https://amzn.to/2I5pCK3

The Hidden Wife: https://amzn.to/2FE5nO3

The Wrong Husband: https://amzn.to/2rfroyw

The Golden Lie: https://amzn.to/2FDiwXM

The Janes: https://amzn.to/2rhnCUl

Your Pastor My Husband: https://amzn.to/2rgDG96

For autographed paperbacks or writing services visit:

www.authorbmhardin.com

To contact: E-mail: bmhardinbooks@gmail.com

Made in the USA
Columbia, SC
26 December 2019